Confessions of an Office Worker
before, during and after a pandemic

Confessions of an Office Worker before, during and after a pandemic

Kieron J R Crowther

Matador
Unit E2 Airfield Business Park,
Harrison Road, Market Harborough,
Leicestershire. LE16 7UL
Tel: 0116 2792299
Email: books@troubador.co.uk
Web: www.troubador.co.uk/matador
Twitter: @matadorbooks

ISBN 978 1803134 796

British Library Cataloguing in Publication Data.
A catalogue record for this book is available from the British Library.

Printed and bound in Great Britain by 4edge Limited
Typeset in 12pt Adobe Garamond Pro by Troubador Publishing Ltd, Leicester, UK

Matador is an imprint of Troubador Publishing Ltd

To my wife, my daughter, my family and to Keyworkers worldwide

Oh and to Jim from accounts…

Part 1

1

The Fall

There are few things in life as embarrassing as falling over in a public place. People stare. It's human nature to want to watch other people's misfortune. Deep down everyone is just thankful that it isn't them. Usually, my first thought would be to get up as quickly as possible, act like nothing has happened, and just hope no-one has noticed. But then, there is the odd occasion when you just have to admit defeat.

This may just be one of those occasions.

As I lie here staring into a rain heavy sky, and in quite a bit of pain in my lower back and radiating into my left buttock, having just gone arse over tit in a public place, the first thought that comes to my mind is maybe not the most obvious one in the current circumstance. *Where exactly do Helium Balloons end up when they go into the sky?* That is my first thought. It isn't; *I need to get up immediately and hope no-one has seen me.* It isn't; *Am I hurt?* or *Will I be late for work?* It isn't; *Will Noah be capable of prising himself away from flirting with the purple haired lady for just a few seconds to check on my welfare?* It isn't; *Have I spilt my coffee on my suit and in about ten seconds will be getting hot water burns around my groin region?* No, it isn't any of these things. I am thinking about balloons. And then I am thinking, *maybe this is about as rock bottom as I can get?* Physically, mentally, spiritually, emotionally.

My name is Maxwell Orwellian. I am about forty-one years and seven months of age. I work in an office. So that makes me an office worker by trade. I have been an office worker pretty much all my working life. My dad was an office worker, and his dad before him. You might say that the office worker baton had been passed down through the generations in my family. Apart from my great grandad, who sold coat hangers.

I have a daughter with my ex called Evie. She is nineteen. I don't see her anywhere near as much as I would like. I don't have, or have any real need for pets. I have less mates than I used to and only two real friends. I have forty-six friends on Facebook but only know three of them.

In terms of my appearance I have still got most of my own hair and teeth. My hearing and eyesight are still quite good for my age. I don't have any real passion to join an online dating website though. I drink in moderation, but do occasionally binge.

But right now, at this exact moment in time, on a really cold icy day in England in late 2019, the only fact that matters is that I am currently lying just outside the coffee house, just a short walk from the office, and with my body and ego quite badly bruised from having slipped on a patch of ice just outside the door to the coffee house. I am lying fairly straight on the path, with my head about a foot or so from the door, in my work suit, and slightly afraid to move unless I make any injury I might have sustained worse.

The quaint little bell on the door of the coffee house rings. It is a dainty, almost apologetic ring. Like the bell to some old backstreet coffee house. Hold on – that would make sense. This *is* an old backstreet coffee house. The coffee house door opens. It's Noah.

"You OK, Maxwell?"

"Do I look OK, Noah? Someone needs to grit your exit," I reply.

"No need to be rude, my friend. What happened?" Noah asks.

"Well, I know what didn't happen. You coming out to help me back up, or check whether I am OK after falling just outside *your* coffee house – that didn't happen. As for what did happen. Well, I have just fallen over. I might have damaged my head."

"Not much to damage there Maxwell. And sorry, Max, but I had customers to serve. Gottastay professional. As much as you might like to think it might, the world of commerce isn't going to stop spinning just because you had a few too many drinks last night and can't stay on your feet. And if I had to break off and help every punter who falls outside this place we would be out of business pretty soon."

"Customers to serve, my arse. You had customers to flirt with, that's what you had. I should sue."

"You can do Max. I don't own the place, as you well know. Otherwise I wouldn't be working here would I? And also, Maxwell, however well we know each other, I am not going to perform CPR on you in any circumstances. That, my friend, is simply not going to happen."

The quaint little bell hanging over the door of the coffee house rings again. The door opens.

"Oh, sorry," a female voice says. A female in really long, fairly scary looking stilettos. It is incredible how loud the sound of stilettos are when you are lying on the pavement.

"Oh gosh, are you OK?" It is the purple-haired lady that Noah had been flirting with in my hour of need. If I wasn't at rock bottom a minute ago, I am now.

"Don't mind him," Noah says. "I will make sure he gets all the help he needs."

She laughs, but she doesn't stop to help. Am I invisible or something? I could be paralysed.

"Anyway, Max my friend, I would get up if I were you, otherwise you will be late for work. Good thing you hit your head and nothing softer." Noah laughs at his own unfunny joke.

"OK, Max. All joking aside, do you need a hand back to your feet?" he says, offering me his outstretched hand.

I think for a second. Yes, I think I probably do…

I think I might have needed a hand up for a while to be honest.

2

Counting Sheep

I don't think the first time I considered counselling was immediately after my divorce, even though that was traumatic enough. It also wasn't immediately after my daughter started blaming me for splitting up with her Mother. It wasn't even when a couple of students ploughed into the back of the new car I had just bought, for the first time ever without the help of a car loan or any kind or cheap finance arrangement. No, it wasn't actually any of these things.

It was when I was sat at home alone, quite a few months after my divorce, listening to one of Bob Marley's most uplifting classic tunes "Two Little Birds", and then finding myself giving Bob the bird. You know you are in a little bit of a bleak place when you are questioning the Marley family and their outlook on the world. I decided then that I might need a bit of help. Counselling, talking therapy, psychotherapy, whatever the correct terminology was. That kind of thing. Maybe just a few sessions. Just someone to talk to really, to bounce some quite personal stuff off. To exorcise some demons, if there were any floating around. Not that I was quite at any kind of full breakdown stage.

My first taste of any kind of therapy had come from an unlikely source many years ago. It was from Ivan the pisshead. Ivan the pisshead was the local regular in my pub from a few years back. A full-blooded alcoholic. Not a trained or accredited therapist by any stretch of the imagination. I was in a stage of my life when I was in my local most nights. I was probably also drinking a little too much in that period. Not quite at that point in Ivan's league but just about enough for me to hold my own in conversations with him.

Something he said stayed with me.

"You know what you gotta do mate" Ivan said, one night when he was particularly off his face on Vodka.

"No Ivan, what would that be then?" I said.

"Good question Maxwell glad you asked" slurring his words quite a bit. "So what you gotta do is this. You gotta shrink the gap."

"Shrink the gap Ivan?"

"That's it, you've got it already. Shrink the gap"

"What gap Ivan?"

"You know, the *gap*."

At this point I recall I was about to call it a night.

But for some reason I held on.

"Ivan, I don't know what gap I am supposed to be shrinking. You've gotta spell it out for me. Pretend I am some kind of idiot" I say.

"Ok I can do that Maxwell. So the gap that you must shrink is between the shit that goes on in the actual world" Ivan said, at the same time lifting up and shaking his left hand to signify the actual world,

"… and your own view of what the world should be" Ivan carried on now holding up and shaking his right hand.

"The further the gap, the unhappier a person becomes. The closer the gap, well my friend, *that* is where happiness lies."

It took me a few seconds to process what Ivan the pisshead had just said. Obviously anything sounds uplifting and profound when you are on your fifth pint of lager, but even in that slightly euphoric state what Ivan said had really taken me by surprise. And not because Ivan fell off his stool just a couple of seconds later having face-planted the bar. It took me aback because he was particularly right in that statement. The therapy seeds were I think sown for me in that moment. I just didn't quite realise it.

Therapy wasn't encouraged when I was growing up. In fact I don't even think it existed when I was growing up. But I thought I would give it a punt. After a fair bit of time in the mental wilderness and getting pissed a little too often for my liking, I figured it couldn't hurt.

So that is why I happen to be sat in Lennox's waiting room at about 1.05pm, over my lunch break from work. I found Lennox on the internet. I don't even know his surname. He was just listed under "Lennox's Counselling and Wellbeing Centre". The name struck a chord with me. I liked the name Lennox. A strong name. I did make sure he was accredited by whatever governing body governs counsellors and all that. Truth be told, I probably should have gone a bit further and got references and double-checked accreditations and generally just done a bit more 'due diligence' on Lennox. Letting someone into the darkest recesses of your mind is not a trivial matter. But apart from the strong name, I think I chose Lennox because he had a consulting room about two minutes from the office; convenience was a big consideration.

I try to ensure I have at least one session a week with Lennox, which is normally on a Wednesday or a Friday, shoehorned into my lunchtime break.

Today there is some relaxing music playing in the reception area. Actually, there is always some relaxing music playing. I am rummaging through the reading material on the table. It is a curious mix of health and lifestyle magazines and, for some reason, comic books. I have never quite worked out whether the comic books are for the children of clients waiting to see Lennox, or actually for the clients themselves. I am currently reading the *Beano*.

The counselling room door opens with some gusto.

"Ah, Maxwell, come through. Sorry I am a bit late," Lennox says, sounding slightly flustered. For a counsellor, and on that basis a man who should generally portray calmness and tranquility, Lennox does sometimes get a bit flustered.

"No problem, Lennox."

I go in and sit on the counselling sofa. This sofa must be the most comfy sofa ever. It is the kind of sofa you assume is only supplied to counselling suites. Like collapsing into a pool of marshmallows.

"So how are you, Maxwell?"

"Yeah, not too bad, Lennox. Trying to work on the bits we talked about last time."

"Ah yes. So how have you found that?" Lennox says. "Err… so actually, Lennox, I can't quite remember the homework you set for me last week," I say apologetically.

These counselling sessions are like being back at school. You have homework to do. I prefer the talking bits. I struggle with the homework. I never really liked homework at school and didn't really think I would be doing it the wrong side of forty. I think Lennox had set me some form of muscle relaxation technique from last week. Something for the mind and body.

"Sorry Lennox, just been so busy with work and everything."

"No worries, Maxwell. So we can just go through some more general stuff today. Maybe use this session as a bit of a talking shop. Just an opportunity for you to talk about what's on your mind generally," Lennox says.

"OK, that's fine."

"So how are you actually doing, Maxwell? I mean, how are you *really* doing?"

I think for a second.

"Actually, Lennox… so I think I may have been struggling a bit more than usual in the last few weeks if I am honest."

"OK. That's all OK. That's partly why you are here. My job would be pretty easy if you weren't ever struggling," Lennox says in his usual reassuring fashion.

"So tell me a little more about how you are feeling, then. At what is bothering you most at the moment. Is it personal? Work issues?"

"Not sure really. Obviously there are the wider issues. We know about them. We have been through them a fair bit."

Those 'wider issues', I think, are all to do with, in no particular order, a failed marriage, a slightly estranged daughter, a lack of progression at work, and the fact that, however many pairs of work socks I buy, I never seem to be able to find a pair that match.

"Insomnia in a word Lennox. That's what my biggest problem is at the moment. I am getting far too much insomnia and far too little sleep at the moment."

"Not uncommon, Max, that in actual fact. Sleep problems that is. Many of my clients who have any form of anxiety often have trouble sleeping. It becomes a bit of a vicious circle though. And a pretty hard one to break at that. So how long has this been going on for you?"

"Well I would like to say it is a recent problem, but to be honest, and give or take a year or so, probably about two years. But it has been really bad in the last few weeks."

Lennox looks at me with a look that smacks of 'Fucking hell, seriously?' "I know, I know. You don't need to tell me that this isn't good. I know that you need sleep to regenerate the soul and all that. That's part of the problem. I don't relax. The doctor wont prescribe sleeping pills – something to do with addiction or something. Anyway, between 2 and 4am, that's usually my worst time. And then in the morning at about seven, when I have to get up, I could sleep like a baby."

"And that obviously makes you tired during the day I would imagine?"

"Dog-tired usually, Lennox. Dog-tired."

"Do you try any techniques to get you to sleep?"
"Yes, I have a few. I start with watching TV, or YouTube videos. But to be honest that just makes me more awake."

"It will do, Maxwell. Your brain thinks you are awake when you put screens all over the place. Anything else?"

"Well, it may be a bit of a cliché… and it might be only for children…"

"Go on."

"I sometimes count sheep."

"OK, and does that work for you?" Lennox asks.
"Not really. I have this issue with sheep number fifteen."

"Sheep number fifteen?" Lennox asks with a slightly concerned face. I don't think he dealt with this one in therapy school.

"Yes, sheep number fifteen."

"So what happens to sheep number fifteen?" Lennox asks.

I hesitate. I haven't ever told anyone about sheep number fifteen before. Not even Lennox – not even a professional who has gone through years of training to deal with people like me.

"Sheep number fifteen never gets over the fence," I say.

"Why not?" Lennox asks. His usual calm and placid demeanor is rapidly being replaced by an increasing look of bewilderment.

"So sheep number fifteen always gets stuck on the fence. Actually probably a bit more than gets stuck. Impaled, really. That then causes a bit of a pile-up of sheep behind sheep number 15."

"OK, that's interesting, Maxwell. Is it always sheep number fifteen?"

"Yes," I say.

"OK. There might be some significance there. Might be one to revisit."

Lennox might be over-analysing this one. The simple answer might be that I am just a bit shit at counting sheep. He must be dying to call me some kind of deranged mentalist at this point. Ever the professional though.

"So on the assumption that you can't sleep, what do you do between two and four in the morning?"

I pause for a second. *What do I do?*

"So the other day I ate a whole bunch of grapes at about 2am."

There is quite a long pause. Maybe Lennox has taken too much at this point.

"I must confess that is a new one on me, Maxwell." Thought that might be the case.

"So you know that as soon as you eat, your body thinks you are awake and your digestive system starts kicking in, which reduces your chances of getting back to sleep?"

I didn't know that actually. But that's why I pay Lennox the dollar. To point that kind of stuff out. It might be obvious sometimes, but it still needs pointing out.

"But the thing is, Lennox, I am not sure there is any deep-seated reason for it. I just got into a bad habit of getting up in the middle of the night, finding myself with nothing to do, mainly because it is the middle of the night, and then opening the fridge. It became a bit of a habit. Some nights I don't even know I am doing it. But having said all that... and I know this might be a bit weird but, well food just tastes that bit nicer in the middle of the night."

Lennox laughs.

I laugh also, but not really because it is funny. It's a polite laugh, laughing along with Lennox. I'm not sure I was joking... food does taste better in the middle of the night.

3

Wendy

To say that life in the twenty-first century is about social media is to state the obvious. Some call it anti-social media. That's probably more accurate. But whatever it is called, it is everywhere. People posting. People replying to posting. People desperate for followers. People following other people. People desperate for subscribers. People subscribing. People tweeting. People replying to tweets. People frantically trying to delete tweets. TikTok. Meta. Facebook. You can't get away from any of it. Well, you can actually. I could burn my phone. I remember the days that I used to tell my daughter to put her phone away. I quickly realised that was a fight I would never win.

Then there is the live, real-time, twenty-four-hour news. Live news. Live updates. Sometimes news before the news has even happened. Just a barrage of information. Information overload. Probably a lot of misinformation also.

I succumbed. My grandmother was ninety-four when she died. But even she was on TikTok before her passing, God bless her. So the first thing I do when I wake up in the morning at about 6.30, when the room is all dark, is not to get up, put the light on and go to the bathroom. No, the first act of the day is to find my mobile. Before anything else, I need to feel where my phone is. Which is why I am currently whacking my arms around the bed in the darkness to feel for it. Where is it? Where is it? Bastard. Not down the crack in the bed. At least twice a week my phone ends up down the crack. Even if I put it on my bedside cabinet, it still ends up down the crack in my bed. The only way of truly knowing why would be to install a CCTV feed in my bedroom, and then dedicating a whole day to watch the footage back. But that would probably not be the best idea. There are some things in this world that you just don't want to know.

I breath a sigh of relief. There it is. I can feel the unmistakably oblong feel of the phone. Back in my hand. I am holding it in my hands. My window to the world. I feel like half a person without it.

Before I have a chance to check the news, I suddenly feel a blow to the face. It knocks the phone out of my hand.

"Maxwell, get up, you lazy git. I am sure you are getting later and later for work by the day."

"Wendy, I am up. Look. My eyes are open." I open them really wide to make a point, slightly straining the right one as I do.

"What you are doing, my lovely, is dicking around on your phone. You are going to get bed sores if you stay in bed much longer. And I am not applying any cream to any part of your body if that happens. I don't care how long we have known each other."

"Blimey Wendy, give me a break. You must have the time wrong. I have at least another fifty minutes."

"No Max, you don't. It is nearly 9am."

Shit, Wendy is right. It is 8.25am, not 7.25am. Bollocks. I have missed the 8.08 train. I can't be late for work. I get that from my upbringing. From a very young age punctuality was instilled in me. As much as doing my Maths, or brushing my teeth. Being late for work in my mind means a lack of discipline and a poor and disorganised lifestyle that brings you to the attention of your immediate bosses. That in turn leads to disciplinary action and the possible sack from your current employer. A lack of any meaningful references means no other employers will take you. That leads to no money, and being forced to eat out-of-date food because it is the only thing you can afford. That, in the end, leads to illness, obesity, premature aging, and ultimately, death. So, for those reasons, I try to avoid being late.

"Yes, OK, you have a point actually. Give me some space then, I am not even sure I am decent," I say to Wendy as I stand up, trying to pull the sheets over me.

"I have seen you before in your birthday suit, remember. There are no secrets there."

"Yeah, when we were about six years old."

"Not much has changed, Maxwell," Wendy laughs. I throw a pillow at her with my spare hand.

"See you tonight Maxwell. Love you."

Fuck me I am really late today.

4

The Notebook

The tie is an integral part of getting ready for any day in the office. Nothing says 'office worker' more than the tie. Most pieces of clothing that have ever been invented have some kind of purpose. Maybe to keep us warm. Maybe to keep us dry and comfortable. Even one of the greatest crimes against fashion, the male open-toe sandal, does at least have some use if you are on a beach. But the tie? What's its job? What's its function? Does it have a function or is it about what it stands for? The suit and tie is the trademark, the symbol of the office worker across the world.

In my office the only time that you can get away with not wearing a tie is when the hot-weather policy applies. The hot-weather policy is basically when the temperature tops thirty degrees Celsius. That means just about never if you live in the North of England.

Putting on the tie is also still a problem for me even after about twenty years. Most people generally get quite good at things that they've done more than a thousand or so times. Not me putting on a tie. Through Boy Scouts to school, then university graduation photos and into the workplace. I still don't really know how to do it. I have never really got the length of the tie right. It ends up being either too low or too high, or the under tie is too far down. Too tight on the neck, too loose on the neck. Over the years, how I have worn my tie has probably been a bit of a barometer for my mood. Nice, tight, clean knot and perfectly matching shirt, and all is generally well. Loose knot, incorrect tie length and food stains, and things are generally less rosy.

For my commute to work I usually like to travel light as far as possible. First no bag. Of any description. Some office workers do. But I don't want to look like Jack the Ripper's great-grandson, so I choose not to have one. Wallet, keys, iPad and – of course – my mobile. Some office workers prefer their watches. Watches that allow every office worker to monitor every bodily function. Every skipped heartbeat. Every bit of raised blood pressure. If you are in the office private medical insurance scheme, these watches are standard issue. I'm not. In any private medical scheme, that is. So I don't need a watch. I don't want a watch that tells me that I've only done ten steps today and therefore I might be at risk of diabetes. I want a real doctor with a current practising certificate to tell me when my time might be nearly up, not some faceless computer strapped to my wrist.

As part of more recent daily routine, I have built in a couple of minutes to write in my notebook. I have a battered old notebook. I have had it for years. The old school type with faint lines. The front is ripped and there is some sticky substance on the top left. God only knows what that is. I think Lennox encouraged me to start writing stuff down a little while ago. Not a diary in the conventional sense. I am no Adrian Mole. But Lennox said to me, and I think I recall this correctly, "Write shit down." I think it may be the one and only time he has ever sworn. That's why I remember it. There is nothing in this world more alarming than someone who never swears, swearing. And it has even more impact when it is a therapist. But when it happens, it carries weight. What Lennox was saying to me, I believe, is to capture my thoughts. Writing stuff down is… what is the word? Cathartic. Something like that. A good way to get the demons out if there are any hiding away. So I have been writing stuff down.

I don't write anything too long-winded or too involved. Just short stuff. More in the way of thoughts. My thoughts for the day. Could be my own. Could be stuff I hear other people say. Or an idea. It could be an idea. Sometimes it might be as basic as my shopping list. A bit of poetry thrown in. Maybe I am a frustrated poet. A frustrated writer. The notebook is where I hide my thoughts. A stream of consciousness, or a stream of shit. I don't really know what it is. So it must be art.

5

The Plow

I get the train to work. I have done pretty much all my working life. My local commuter out-of-town train station is a fairly terrifying place. As far away from the toy train stations of my childhood as you can get, with the friendly train conductor figures. The reality of this station is a long way from that. It is about as welcoming as a desert in the middle of a heatwave. It is just a mass of stone and concrete, like something out of a 1970s English tower block. There are occasional bits of life, like some half-ripped posters advertising films that were last in the cinema about three years ago.

There are never any workers at my local station. It doesn't matter what time of day it is. There is never anyone here in any form of working capacity. No one picking rubbish up. No community support workers. No security. It's like the apocalypse just happened, with this station at the epicentre.

There are no bins on this station either. To my mind, bins are necessary for a civilised society. The world is truly mobile now. Not only do people surf and browse on their phones, mobiles, tablet, whatever it might be when on the move, they also eat on the move.

I think it used to be considered a bit slovenly. Not so much these days.

It isn't often that I do, but if I ever fancy a banana, an injection of potassium to get me fired up for the working day, there isn't a bin to discard the banana skin in when I get there. As I understand it, the lack of bins is for security reasons. To avoid bombs being left in bins by terrorists. I don't think this station would be high on any terrorist's hit list. It would probably be improved by a controlled demolition anyway.

Then there are the station signs. Station signs are everywhere. Each one suggestive of an imminent risk of death. The one to my right has the blacked-out silhouette of a man falling to his death from the bridge over the station with a big red cross through the middle. I think that means either a lack of suitable railings on the bridge or, more likely, a risk of suicide. Either way, I don't think that a sign is the best deterrent to someone in that kind of state of mind. The continuous yellow line at the edge of the platform is a strange one – with an accompanying sign of a man being electrocuted. What kind of person voluntarily runs across train tracks? Signs are just everywhere on this station. The only sign missing, I think, is the United Nations sign for mines in the area.

Today it is around 8.02am on a fairly cold, frosty office morning. I like to give myself time to spare to get to the station, just on the off-chance that the 8.08 is early for once. I generally try to avoid ending up running for the train, as, in addition to all the reasons for not being late, this can mean running in an office suit and tie. People tend to stare at people running in suits, and sweating whilst wearing a suit in an office all day is not desirable for anyone sitting close to me at work.

People start to arrive about 8.05am. First is the 'couple'. In this instance it is a woman and a man. She is always fairly smartly dressed. He generally isn't. But they are always holding hands. I have no issues with the holding of hands, even if it is in a public place. Real lovebirds. I remember when I was like that. What they mustn't do, though, under any circumstances and at any stage, is to swing their arms in unison when holding hands. That needs to be kept indoors.

Next to arrive at the station is the 'beatboxer'. This chap is a suited and booted office worker in the true sense of the word. Nice tailored suit, shiny shoes, always well- groomed, hair always in place – but always with massive silver headphones strapped to his ears. Big steel drums over both ears as headphones. No little compact air pods. No subtlety here whatsoever. Also not the more acceptable Beats-branded headphones. No, this chap goes large and shiny with his audiological equipment. Today is no exception. There he is, sauntering into the station, half dancing, half walking. But the steel drums are just a bizarre look. Like a clash of worlds. Sensible office worker below, but with a nightclub on his head.

When you stand close to the track you can see the train coming from miles off. Literally for about two miles on the straight track. Just as the crow flies. No kinks or curves. I check my phone – the one I will shortly be impressing my office co-workers with. It won't be long now.

There you go. Here she comes. The small dot on the horizon signifies the impending arrival of the commuter train. It is never to be taken for granted. Often the train is delayed or cancelled, usually for signalling issues or animals on the line. You have to accept that trains in England are on time less than they are not. We aren't in Tokyo.

That also means one other commuter hasn't yet joined the party. Where is he? Oh, here he comes. Like clockwork. Clockwork at always being late that is. It is just bizarre. The perennially late office worker (or PLOW, for short) comes bolting round the corner, tie half done, one shoelace flopping, trousers half hanging down his arse, flies undone, sweaty and red-faced as usual. This guy is late every day, or nearly every day. I can't work out if his timing is exemplary, or really bad. He always makes it with about thirty seconds left to go. It is as if he gets some sexual pleasure out of being late. He takes it to the wire just about every day.

The PLOW makes life even harder for himself by never having a ticket. Most people who take the train regularly worked out a few years ago that getting an advance rail card makes sense, financially and practically. It is cheaper, and it takes the ball-ache out of getting a ticket every day. But even though the PLOW is here just about every day of his life, even though he never has the time, he always gets a ticket from one of the ticket machines. The ticket machines on this platform are usually out of paper, vandalised, or out of order. Here he goes again today, frantically chucking some loose change into the ticket machine, anxiously looking towards the track for the train. God bless him.

I always like to try to focus on the train driver as the train pulls up. Every day I look into the cockpit (or whatever the equivalent is in train terminology), searching for some flicker of emotion from the driver. There are generally different drivers most days. Occasionally it is the same driver. But all have one thing in common: absolutely no fucking eye contact. None. They simply don't want to know. You would think that pulling into the station would be breaking up the sheer boredom of looking at miles upon miles of track. But no. There is nothing. I could be standing there stark naked from the waist down and still there would be nothing. Still not a flicker. The cockpit of the train is their place of work, their equivalent of the office, but maybe with a little less stationery.

6

Jim from Accounts

"Maxwell! Hey, Max, wait up!" comes an all-too-familiar voice from behind me as I am just about to board the train. Oh dear. I was looking forward to a nice, chilled train journey. The voice is that of Jim. Jim who works in our office. Jim from the Accounts department. He is an occasional commuter on the 8.08 commuter train. Jim is quite honestly just completely wrapped up in his own world. His own world of numbers and figures. It isn't his fault. He doesn't know much better. His father and his father before him were probably accountants. He is only truly happy when he is counting something I suspect. Personally, I have nothing against Jim. It is more his profession I have the issue with. I don't get numbers. I never have. So people who work around numbers and Excel spreadsheets are an alien concept to me. I think I would rather meet the neighbourhood gang in a dark alley late at night on a commute home from the office than Jim from Accounts. But here I am again. And Jim has well and truly rumbled me.

"Jim," I reply, trying to sound pleased to see him, "How are you?"

"Yes, can't complain, can't complain. You got a busy

day ahead?" he says with his usual breathtaking level of optimism.

"Yeah, I have a few meetings, Jim," I say.

"Ah good, that's good. Got loads on today. Team meeting first thing and then we have got the external auditors coming in later. Should be OK though. We have been putting in new internal processes in the last few weeks to get us ahead of the game with the auditors…"

My mind wanders, thoughts turning already to what I should have for dinner tonight.

Jim continues. "And then I think the new software will be really game-changing for the firm. Genuinely, I believe that. I think management really showed some nerve and foresight in investing in the platform. What do you think?"

"Yeah, definitely agree with that," I say without having a clue what he is talking about.

"Ah good, good, yes. It will make all the staff more connected with Accounts."

All I can hope for now is that the conversation will get lost in the commuter rush to board the train. I move to the doors, trying to get lost in the crowd. Jim moves with me. He's still talking…

Please, let there not be just double seat spaces left on the train. That would mean having to talk to Jim the whole trip to work. I just want a bit of clear headspace before work. Just give me some single spaces, preferably a few seats apart. Where are they? I frantically scan the train seating system. Of course there are plenty of double spaces. Oh joy upon joy. I sit down. Jim sits down next to me. The conversation that ensues with Jim is beyond the scope of this book.

7

Morning coffee

There must be at least fifteen coffee houses within a one-mile radius of the office. They are everywhere. Commercial ones, small independents, trendy student ones. It doesn't matter how many spring up, they always end up well used. And a good proportion of the customers are office workers.

But the thing about the coffee house is that it isn't actually about the coffee. Not anymore. Coffee houses have become more than the coffee. The coffee house has become a meeting point. Mini gatherings. Leisurely catch-ups over coffee at lunch. One-on-one lunches. Corporate power breakfasts. But amongst all the socialising, corporate bonding and probably even first dates, the coffee houses are really the only place that you can go to on your own, power up a laptop or whip out a book or iPad, and proceed to spend anywhere between two and eight hours there without being labelled a sad and pathetic loner. No one rushing you from a table. No reservations. There is no sign on the wall limiting your stay or your return. Buying a coffee basically rents you a seat, and some free heating and free WiFi into the bargain. For a whole day if you want. Coffee houses have become a hotbed for office workers. They're like bees on a lavender plant dripping in honey. The 'in' place. A place to lunch. A place to network. A place to interview other prospective office workers. A place to sack office workers. You can bring just about anything with you into these coffee houses – laptops, iPads, calculators, pens and papers. All the stuff that the office worker needs. I have even seen someone set up a desktop in a coffee house, and ask the staff for an extension lead. You could bring your whole office to the coffee house if you were so inclined.

Imagine if restaurants worked like this. If, after your pudding, instead of the free mint and being politely asked to leave the table – after your bill with an optional 20% service charge is added automatically – you just set your stall out at the restaurant table, hunker down with an aperitif and only leave when you are good and ready. Not happening.

I have been swept up by this. Maybe because I have recently been spending a lot of time on my own. Anywhere where this isn't really noticed is welcome. I don't even think I like coffee all that much. Many a time I have got to my office desk with a puzzled look on my face, staring at my caffeine-filled plastic cup and thinking of all the other things in life that £4.95 could've bought. Five coffees a week at an average price of £4 per day. That's £800 a year. Over about 12 years that's nearly £12,000. Just on a drink. I could have bought a car for that price, and one that's done less than 30,000 miles to boot. And the coffees themselves are exploding. Add ons and extras are in fashion. Gone are the days where the choice was black or white coffee. Maybe the occasional green tea here and there. No, now it is all about the extras, the add ons, the combos. The option of an injection of vitamins. Vitamins in a coffee? You can mix it up with the ice cream latte with vitamins, zinc and marshmallow. Or the ice cream sorbet, coconut and strawberry cappuccino with an extra shot of Vitamin D. With all the add ons and variants, and going large, you could be pushing the £10 mark in some of these places. That isn't a drink. That is a meal. Even the loyalty apps won't be saving you from financial ruin.

8

Part I

Noah and the Alien Jury

As far as possible, I tend to avoid the main commercial coffee houses. Just down a little side street about two streets away from my office is a little independent. There aren't many other shops on the street. It has been – and still is, as far as I know – run by some former students who studied coffee bean-ology, or whatever the correct description is, when on a gap year somewhere in the Amazonian rainforest. I have never actually seen them. But Noah works here. Noah is the chap who didn't give me a hand up when I stacked it outside the coffee house. But he also, probably an unlikely best mate. He has worked here for just about as long as I have been at the office. And that means a lot of chat over morning coffee's over a year. Generally the conversation is a bit superficial, as blokey chat often is. But then he has also seen me at my lowest.

As I open the door, the familiar little apologetic internal bell rings. The décor is a bit... well, what you might call a bit basic. A bit wooden. Earthy. It is all wooden tables and chairs. Quite unpleasant if you are sitting in there for a long period. But it is quiet, and before a long day in the office, that will do for me.

"Maxwell, my friend, good morning!" Noah comes out the back of the shop. "Just on a bathroom break, Maxwell."

"I hope you have washed your hands before you serve me then."

Noah is always that half-a-glass-full kind of chap. The kind of person who thinks you could empty the ocean with a spoon if you put your mind to it. My glass of milk hasn't been much fuller than 50% in the last year or so. After my divorce it probably went down to about 28% full. Maybe with a marginal 1% rise month on month since then. Lennox has been looking into that with me, trying to get that statistic going in the right direction.

"The usual, Max, my friend?"

"Yes please, fella. Actually, Noah, what is my usual?" "Let me tell you what your usual is. Your usual, my friend, with some of the finest coffee beans sourced from some of the remotest regions of the world available in this establishment, is… either a cappuccino or a latte. You can travel the coffee bean world in this place and you choose to go for one of them two. Says a lot about a man does that."

"Oh, yes. That's right. So I will have my usual then. Give me a cap. Can you make it a large today though? And if you could empty the jar of chocolate sprinkles onto the top, that would be appreciated."

"Any more theories for me?" Noah says over the sound of the coffee machine as he makes my drink.

Noah and I share a bit of a passion for the weird, really. Just a bit left of centre. Occasionally chatting about the kind of stuff that you couldn't really bring up at a dinner party. Noah started it a few months ago. I blame him. If I recall, he just casually threw into the conversation that he thought that we were all the by-product of some form of alien science experiment. Since then we have started to talk all kinds of stuff. Alien invasions. Conspiracy theories. Stuff to do with space. Probably the kind of stuff that would mean I could hold my own with the local wino on the street clutching a bottle of White Lightning on a Saturday night.

"So, Noah," I say as he passes me my drink with a complimentary biscuit on the side. "Here's my thought for the day. Now bear with me on this one." I pause. I'm not so sure if even Noah can handle this one. "So, this is my thought for the day. You don't exist. *I* don't exist. What I am seeing all around me – this coffee shop, you, the really nice biscuit you are about to give me complimentary with my coffee as a regular – none of this is real. It's some gigantic computer programming a world around us. And beyond what I can see, or should I say what I am programmed to see, is actually… well, just nothing. Blankness. Whiteness. A bit like on the edge of space."

I may be losing him on this one. I am starting to lose momentum myself.

"That's a really good one," Noah finally replies. "But the problem with that one is this: if you don't think my coffee exists, then why have you just ordered one? A bit more thought next time, my friend."

"What about this one for a bit more thought: I am writing a book."

Noah's face goes from slight perplexion to hilarity. "Get the fuck out of town, Maxwell. What about? The history of this coffee shop? I would buy that. Anything else I want for free. And anyway, if your last theory is true then you aren't writing the book; the big, gigantic computer in the sky somewhere is writing it for you!"

He has a point there.

"That may be true, but I am still writing it. I'm up to 30,000 words at the moment. It's called *The Alien Jury*," I say. "I'm not bullshitting. I have been writing a little bit here, a little bit there. Probably for the best part of the last ten years."

I haven't actually, but Noah doesn't need to know that. I have, though, written the title in my notebook. I have also managed to draw a picture of twelve aliens in a jury dock in a courtroom with a human judge and a human audience.

"Seriously, I have," I say.

"What's it about then? Another *ET*?"

"No. It's nothing to do with sci-fi or weird-looking dogs in a basket. Think about it, Noah. I would expect more from you. As you should get from the title, it's about morality."

"Morality?" Noah says. "Oh, of course, it is so obvious from the title" he says with sarcasm. "What's the connection to aliens then? They don't even have brains as far as I know, let alone any morals. Come on, Max, enlighten me. I am obviously slow off the mark this morning."

"It's about stuff that goes on in the world that, if an alien was sitting next to you looking at that stuff, he would respond by saying, 'What the fuck is that about, how is that fair?' Basically, the alien is some guy who has no idea of anything. No history, no baggage. The alien is the judge. They decide what is fair and not fair. Hence, the Alien Jury."

"Sounds like a bestseller. Listen, as long as it isn't your memoires then it has a chance," Noah laughs. "And I don't want to bring you back down to earth too hard, J K Rowling, but even the most famous authors still have to pay for their coffees. That will be £4.25, please."

8

Part II

The Llama and the Purple-Haired Lady

Still in Noah's coffee house, I have my drink, my seat, and my own thoughts. I have about ten minutes or so before having to make my way to the office. A couple more customers have arrived. Noah is holding court with them. I glance to the far end of the cafe. It doesn't take long as the coffee house is only about ten square metres. There he is again. The regular. I call him the the Jam and Toast man. Because he always has jam and toast. Every time I see him. Jam and toast. And a cup of tea. He always sits in the same seat looking straight out onto the street. He usually has a beanie hat on. Even in summer. And a lumberjack's shirt.

But the way he eats his jam and toast is something to behold. He seems to take some odd indirect route, straight up to mouth height vertically before then travelling horizontally into his mouth. I have never seen anything like it in my life. It is actually fascinating. It is like he has been programmed to eat in the most inefficient way possible. He faces out towards the street. He turns his chair round deliberately to face the road. Just so everyone can see him.

He reminds me of a strong memory from my youth. I was in a zoo. I think I was probably about twelve or thirteen. I must have been with my parents. I remember wandering around looking at all the animals, really interesting animals from all over the world. Most of the animals weren't interested in me. Animals in the zoo are probably a bit bored of people looking at them. But I remember one animal in particular. I think it might have been a llama. Anyway, I remember this animal just staring at my face. It wasn't an innocuous glance. It was a proper stare. It fascinated me. It was like this animal was reading my mind, or trying to connect with me on some cerebral level. Like some portal between the human world and the animal kingdom. For maybe ten seconds, he or she kept my gaze. And then, without any warning whatsoever, it just took a massive dump. I mean huge pellet-like pieces. And it still didn't move. It just stayed motionless, doing it's business. Couldn't give two shits. This chap always reminds me of that llama.

The coffee house doorbell rings again. In comes the purple-haired lady again. The one that Noah was in flirt land with when I fell over outside a few weeks back.

I might have done the same thing though if I was in his position. She is striking. And not just because of her hair. There is something about her. She has high heels on and is very well dressed. But not in a Saturday-night- into-Sunday-morning high heels kind of way.

She has on a suit. A really polished, well presented, well tailored suit. A bit of make-up, but not in the in-your-face, blood-red lipstick kind of way. The *hair* though. Just bright purple. I assume it isn't her natural colour. You don't see bright purple hair everyday. Not with a smart suit anyway.

I smile inwardly. Noah will be on his best behaviour with this lady. Sadly I cant be a voyeur to this though. I need to get to work. It's nearly five to nine. And I need to be in the office shortly. Can't be late.

9

Charlie

I always straighten my tie just before getting to the office. The tie is always a bit looser for the commute; now is the time to just tighten it a notch. And there she is. My office. The office is a huge big glass building. There are about ten floors in the building. It probably houses around one thousand office workers. I don't know most of them. This is no small office. And this is just one of the regional offices. This is a big beast of a corporate machine.

The foyer is big, lavish, modern. A large expanse. This is the area that visitors see. That means that this is the area that the most money is spent on. It didn't used to be that way. Years ago the foyer was just like a massive broom cupboard. Not anymore, though. There are TV screens all over with Sky News and live stock market updates on. Plush velvet sofas all around – the sofas that visitors to the office will sit on, never for office workers themselves. Not unless they are entertaining customers at the same time. There are scented candles on the desk, rainbow-coloured lava lamps dotted around the reception. All a nod to Management trying to make the office… well, a bit less of an office, and a bit more contemporary. And there, in the middle of it all, sits Charlie. The office… er, concierge? Not sure really. Receptionist. Security man. The chap who says hello to everyone. Whatever he is, you wouldn't be going far wrong if you described him as the gatekeeper to the office. We all have to pass Charlie on our way in. He has a little boxed-off area in reception behind some glass.

Of all his possible roles, the label 'security man' is probably the most tenuous. Whilst I am not an expert in the field of office security, I would think that one of the essential aspects of being a security guard is actually, to be able to run. But as long as I have known Charlie, he has had some form of strapping on his left foot. I don't know why. I am not sure even he knows. But it seems to me that this strapping would only hinder Charlie's movement if he was suddenly called into action.

But that said, if there was ever a man to do the other part of his job – welcoming people to the building in the morning – it was Charlie. A man capable of talking to anyone, from Management through to the most junior staff. He doesn't care. He's the kind of guy who has seen it all and been there, who has a thousand stories to tell. The only issue is that sometimes, if you are a little short on time in the mornings, you don't want all of those thousand stories in one go.

I genuinely like Charlie though, even though seeing him signifies the start of a working day. The number of times he must have to say 'morning' and 'evening' to office workers is mind-boggling. If there are roughly 1,000 office workers in the building then, barring holidays and people pulling sickies, that is roughly in the region of two thousand times a day he must need to say those words. I couldn't do his job. I would've just put signs up above reception saying 'good morning' and 'have a nice evening'.

"Morning, Maxwell," Charlie says with his enthusiasm. "You got much on today?"

"Yeah probably, Charlie, the usual Monday stuff to try to put off until tomorrow if I can. I'm just going to keep my head down today."

I try not to talk to Charlie about football though. Charlie is obsessed. Get him on football and you won't get away. I must get away so I carry on.

I am in the office lift, one of three in this building, and just about on time. My desk is on the seventh floor, which means I take the lift every day. I am not a fan of the office lifts. If my office was on the third floor, taking the stairs might be more in the running. But the seventh floor is a stretch too far, so the lift is a necessary evil. A bit like the Tube in London. No one wants to take it, to have their face in someone's armpit at 8.38am – or to have their face in someone's armpit at any time of day, for that matter. Lifts are really just small coffin-like boxes with no windows, where people who have usually never met are forced into close physical proximity to each other and feel highly awkward because no one is talking to each other.

It is like being in a taxi and not talking to the driver. At some point, you end up asking the taxi driver if he is busy. In the office lift, it is more a case of who will crack first with the pleasantries. With the bright lift lights and the wraparound mirrors magnifying every facial wrinkle.

These office lifts also have a high tendency to break down. At least one of the three lifts in this building is almost always out of order. This never really inspires confidence in the other lifts. The site of a big yellow cross covering one lift, often with the doors open so you can see just how complicated the engineering is, is not welcoming. And never ever will you find me taking a lift on a Friday evening. A breakdown on a Monday morning can be handled. A breakdown on a Friday evening cannot. The little button with the bell on the lift doesn't, as far as I am aware, connect to the outside world. Your fourth emergency service in the unlikely (but actually very real) possibility that this lift might break down would be an SOS linked directly to Charlie. Charlie can add that role to his CV. But just when you really did need Charlie, he probably wouldn't be there. Your mobile phone obviously wouldn't have any signal, or would have just run out of battery. You would be destined to spend your weekend stuck in a lift. No food and drink for at least fifty hours. Nowhere to relieve yourself. No running water or change of clothes.

The physical recovery from such an event might come in time, after spending several weeks on a drip in hospital, but the mental scars would last a lifetime. It wouldn't matter how good you are at office working or where your office career might've taken you. You would forever be that bloke that got stuck in a lift all weekend. This scenario has played out in my mind on numerous occasions. I can guarantee that this will never happen to me. Never. There is nothing in life that can prepare you for that. There is nothing worse. Maybe being buried alive is in the same ballpark, but at least no one else would know about it. There is one thing that I envisage being worse than being trapped in a lift on a Friday night. And that is being trapped in a lift on a Friday night with Jim from Accounts. That would take me as close to cannibalism as I think I could ever feasibly get.

10

Is it Always a 'Good' Morning?

To climb the greasy office pole, which, metaphorically, runs through this office building, you usually need to become a bit of a dick. Not always. You could stay true to your beliefs and your values. There are some exceptions. But they are few and far between. A wiser man than me, who is also a very experienced office worker, gave me a bit of great advice in my more formative years. "Play the game," he said. "There are always going to be office politics. Don't fight out. Get involved in it. Immerse yourself in it. It is about getting out and about. Keep your office friends close and your office enemies even closer."

I once had a senior manager tell me, also in my formative years, that I actually didn't need to like anyone at work. I didn't need to talk to them or even make them cups of tea. None of that was necessary. There was only one thing that he asked of all his staff. And that was, whatever your mood, however you are feeling, however much you hate any other office worker, you always, *always*, need to say 'good morning' to them. A good portion of my colleagues are 'morning people'. You know, the type of people who, by the time they are sat at their desks, have already been up for five hours, been to the gym, run two miles, and then finished their morning routine off with some yoga, warm-down pilates and meditation. I don't think I am one of them.

This is an open-plan office. Open-plan offices have been the craze for years. Basically everyone is just shoved out in the middle of a big floor, all sat on big banks of tables. It doesn't matter your pay grade or your place in the office pecking order. You're still shoved out in the middle. You can just imagine the protestations from Management when the open plan became a thing. Forced out of the anonymity and secrecy of their own office, often with a plaque on the door with their name on it, and booted out into the middle of the floor with all the plebs.

Open-plan offices have got even more open plan over the years. At the start, all the banks seemed to have partitions. Boards ran upright across each bank of desks so you still had your own little space. But the partitions didn't last long. Who knows where the modern open-plan office will finish? All on the one table? All sharing the same chair?

Open-plan offices have changed the whole dynamic of the office. There is nowhere to hide in an open-plan office. You know what everyone is up to, who they are talking to, if they are even at work in the first place. It is not just the office workers on your immediate bank of four desks. You can hear people even if they are on the other side of the floor. It's as if they have a megaphone on them. Not sure the forefathers and creators of the open-plan office completely thought that bit through. And if you are having a bit of a bad day, even a bit of a bad year, there aren't many hiding places in the open-plan office.

It is nearly 9am. I am not far from my desk now, ambling as I go. I should really be at my desk just before 9am. My career-hungry younger self would be gallivanting to the desk, hungrily saying good morning to anyone who might glance in my direction, and be at my desk ready to work for 8.35am. Not anymore though. I can't be late, but I wont be early either.

My desk is on the last bank of desks right at the end of the floor. I may actually have spent more time in this area than any other in the world, including my bedroom.

"Here he is, the man, the myth, the legend. Morning, Maxwell."

To this day I still don't know if that man is being sincere or sarcastic. That man being Daniel. Daniel sits immediately opposite me, not more than four feet away. Physically the closest office worker to me, but we aren't close in any other sense of the word. It is hard to imagine a more annoying office worker than Daniel. A man who, if God has been given a blueprint to create an office worker to annoy all the other office workers out there, would be the direct result of that experiment. There are no partitions to prevent him from looking directly at me. Just my desktop monitor. That is the only thing between him and me. All day. Every day. Like the kid in school you don't want to be sat next to. So close we could touch

47

if we wanted to, play footsie with each other. We don't though. Choose to touch feet, that is. He also owns his own shopping trolley. Says it all.

Daniel is the only office worker on our bank of four in today. Clare usually sits opposite and to the right. Next to Daniel, poor girl. She is on holiday at the moment though. She takes a lot of holidays. Most people who sit next to Daniel do. Clare is quiet… well, unassuming, maybe a little timid. Nice though. But she is in Magaluf, of all places. I learned from Clare to not let appearances deceive you. She is a right party animal behind the classes and butter wouldn't melt look. She goes to Magaluf every year. Sometimes twice a year. She once told me she's been twenty-five times. Twenty five times? Who has been to Magaluf twenty-five times?

Clive usually sits to my right. He isn't in the office today though. Not sure why. He is usually in about 8.45am. Clive is a stickler for time-keeping, always likes to be ahead of the game. When he is in the office, Clive is always suited and booted. His facial hair is always carefully manicured. I would put Clive in his late fifties. Maybe nearly sixty. His hair is slicked back with thick hair gel. He is your more tailored suit variety of office worker. He seems to have a selection from Savile Row. They are always matching. He's the 007 of the office. The opposite of Daniel in that respect. Like you would imagine a general from the military to be. I think he is one of the few people who has been at this place longer than me.

Clive has a wealth of office worker experience but never quite got to sit at the top table for some reason. I think Management were intimidated by the handkerchief hanging from his pocket. But if he is bothered about that he never seems to show it. This is a man who is a long way through the early office worker arse-kissing phase. The kind of office worker who seems comfortable in his office shoes. He doesn't need to play the office game anymore. He probably wont be going up in the company, but equally he is unlikely to be going down. So that makes for a calm office worker. Someone who is happy in his posh slippers. That also means there's no real edge to him, no office politics to become a part of. And those type of office workers are few and far between. He seems to exude an air of confidence. Slightly suave, a little bit debonaire. A possible candidate for an office affair. Actually, that would be doing him a bit of a disservice. I think he would stop at a bit of flirting.

I think about asking Daniel where Clive is. I think again. I won't get any kind of sensible reply.

I like my desk to be tidy. I always did, although I think I may even be nudging OCD a bit with my desk now. Divorce didn't really help on that front. I have started to line stuff up on my desk. Pens, pencils, the stapler. All need to be nicely parallel and aligned.

OCD about my stapler and desk does, though, fit in quite nicely with the policies Management brought in about a year or so ago. In short, that means no papers, no general debris and no half-eaten food on the desk.

I sit down at my desk once more. Straighten my stapler slightly. Straighten it back again. Check it has staples in it. Sit in the chair that was issued to me when I was but a lowly office worker. My office chair. This chair has been through a lot with me over the years. It is an older make of office chair. In mobile phone terms, it is akin more to an iPhone 1 than the latest model. But it has got through its health and safety MOT over the years. Probably just about scraping through. Over the years it has moulded to my back. No other chair would feel quite the same. Health and Safety have recommended that I upgrade my chair. I have politely told them to shove it up their arses.

Then there is the computer. The PC. In the end, the only piece of equipment that any office worker really needs. In our office, this is still the desktop version. Basically a monitor, the motherboard tower, the keyboard and the mouse. Laptops were issued. But not many. There was a spate of laptops being left on trains, so Management reduced the supply accordingly.

The carpet is a bit of a state, across the office floor generally but especially, for some reason, around my desk. It is the kind of carpet even your great-grandparents would be thinking of replacing – predominantly brown, and generally stained throughout. Generally, and nearly without exception, pretty much every office I have ever seen has brown carpets. Probably for practical reasons. Offices generally equal brown. Brown carpets, brown wallpaper. Just a festival of brown. Doesn't matter how many lava lamps or modern art pieces are placed around the building. Offices always have been, and always will be, brown.

Just under my right chair leg, there is a really large historic stain. I say historic in the sense that as long as I can remember, I think that stain has always been there. I have no idea how it got there. All I knew is that it wasn't me.

There is usually also a small smattering of little bits of hole-punched paper around my chair. Maybe caused by improper use of the hole punch. I have never recalled seeing the discarded little bits of paper floating out of the hole puncher when using it. But somehow, at the end of every day, hundreds of these little bits still seem to litter the floor right around my desk.

Anyway, this is my office area. It has been for the best part of fifteen years or so. Apart from Clive and my office chair, just about everything around me has changed over that time. The people around me have changed quite often. Lots of office workers have left, even more so in the last few years. The desks, the IT equipment – they have all been upgraded and replaced. But for pretty much all of my office career I have occupied this space, on this floor, and of this building. Terrifying when you think about it really.

11

Sean from IT

Today in the office I am finding my mouse is unresponsive to touch. A little blue circle is constantly appearing also. I keep hitting it on the desk to spark it back into action.

"Hey, Maxwell, keep it down please. What's with all that banging?" Daniel pipes up.

"Word's crashed again. Is yours OK?"

"Mine's working fine."

I need to call the IT department. IT is short for Information Technology. No office is complete without an IT department. Even the solitary office worker needs an IT department. No one knows where they are based. I don't recall having met a real-life one of them. There is just a number above everyone's PC next to IT support: 475. It may as well be 666. And it never seems to be the same person. As far as I know, there are hundreds of them. They don't just deal with our office. It all seems very impersonal to me. I still remember the days of the onsite IT helper. Just one chap wandering around with a helpful demeanour and generally telling everyone to switch the PC off and then on again. Those days are long gone. I am on the phone to IT a lot. Usually it is to do with forgetting my password. For the first three months of my working life at this office, I struggled to remember either my username or password. Now I usually forget my password after a holiday. It is always a little bit embarrassing having to phone IT and get them to locate my password and say it back to me. 'Bigdaddy41' is not something you ever really want to say in an open-plan office.

IT don't just fix your computer. They are also in charge of enforcing the Management IT policies. The IT policy generally bans you from visiting porn and gambling sites. Not that I would ever have the urge to do either of them at work, much less in an open-plan office. But over the years, the policy seems to have an ever-increasing number of prohibited websites. Holiday sites, marketplace sites, religious sites. To be honest, they would be better just naming the two websites we *are* allowed to visit.

Anyway, I am confident that I haven't been on any porn sites this morning, and therefore I have a legitimate IT problem.

Today Sean from IT is looking into the issue for me. He will probably need to escalate this to a senior engineer, as usually IT do, but for the time being Sean has well and truly jumped on to my machine and is having a good electronic rummage through my folders. In simple terms, that means Sean has remote connected from wherever he is onto my machine.

In the meantime, whilst he is rummaging around on my PC, I have been checking the state of the stock market on my phone. Cryptocurrency is all the rage across social media. God only knows what that is.

I have been staring at the only picture I have on my desk. That would be me and Evie, my daughter. I have always thought less is more when it comes to office decoration. Some office workers cover their desks in stuff – pictures of their kids, their dogs, their musical influences, their teenage crush. One office worker on the second floor used to have no less than twenty-five pictures of different cats on her partition. Not one human being. A little scary.

So no, I just have this one small picture of me and Evie, in a small frame on my desk. I think we were in the south of France or somewhere like that. It is one of the few photos I have of just Evie and me. She would be about seven I think. The innocence of youth. Not just her. I think I was more innocent then. A young dad. We had Evie pretty early, in our early twenties. I met her mother when we were both just teenagers. I think Evie still somehow blames me for splitting up with her mum. She hasn't said it. But I know. I think I must have messed up being a Dad. But there isn't really any training for it. There are courses for everything now in this world. Everything. From medicine to ping pong, there is a course. But there is not any course on how to be a parent. Why? Probably the most important job on the planet, and no formal training.

Evie is about 19 now. On a gap year with her mates. I try to keep in touch. She doesn't contact me much.

But then again 19 olds probably don't contact their parents much, especially ones that have split up.

"So if you struggle again, just instigate a soft reboot and you should be fine," Sean says.

I just realised I hadn't been listening to a word he has been saying.

12

Trevor and the Office Appraisal

"No, I want to speak to a manager. This is not the first time I have had problems with your products. I had to return a defective kite from your shop last year."

That would be office worker Trevor, then. It is still pretty early on a Friday morning. Around 10.05am. But that never stops Trevor. Trevor is on the phone again. Trevor is loud. Really loud. His sits just about as far away from me as you could get. Right on the other side of the seventh floor. But Trevor seems to distort the laws of sound when he is on the phone. You can hear him as clearly as if he was sitting right next to you. Not only does he not attempt to keep his voice down when on the phone, but he also does not attempt to censor the conversation, even though he is brazenly flouting the office policy of not making personal calls at work. Most right-thinking open-plan office workers attempt to censor their conversation, at least a little bit. But not Trev. He is possibly the least self-conscious man I have ever known. He is up there with the Jam and Toast man from the coffee house.

Today is no exception. He seems to be arguing with a retailer who has sold him some defective goods. The decibel level rises with each word. Here we go. He is building himself up for a full-on tirade in a moment. He is about to blow. I can feel it. You just know every single office worker on the floor is listening to his conversation. And as if to make completely sure that the entire floor hears him today, I think he is also standing up. Standing up and gesticulating with his hands. It is like a one-man soap opera.

"Listen," Trevor carries on, like a dog with a bone. "I don't know what pay grade you are, but I want to speak to an adult capable of making some decisions."

Jesus, he is already getting personal. Whoever he is talking to is having an unbelievably bad day.

"I have better things to be doing than talking to you. I want to know what you are going to do about this."

There is a pause for about a minute. Maybe that is the end of it…

Oh no, not quite.

"Right. That's it. You have left me no choice. Who do I write to with my formal complaint? You haven't heard the last of me, let me tell you!" Trevor finishes his call with a slam of a phone.

2pm

I have been called into an appraisal with HR. HR is short for Human Resources. Hopefully my mate Gertrude will be there. Gertrude Davis is the current head of HR. She was part of my intake into the Company many years ago, then went down the HR route.

I filled out the appraisal form a few weeks ago on the HR intranet site. Each office worker has to rate themselves against each question on a scale of one to five, one being pretty fucking useless to five being Management material in waiting. I generally put down four or five.

There used to be a section on the HR intranet headed 'Employee of the Month'. That was taken down after some incidents of the winner for January of last year being intimidated in the office toilets.

I have a lunchtime coffee in hand. I need a coffee to get through just about any meeting in the office, and the appraisal is no exception. I suppose I had better knock.

"Come in, Maxwell."

This is new. Gertrude is there. But there is someone else also. Some chap in a suit, wearing glasses. Small. Not much hair. Laptop on the desk. Not making any eye contact with me as I walk in.

"Hi Maxwell," Gertrude says. "Take a seat. Long time, no see."

"Yes, hi Gertrude."

The other chap still doesn't look up from his laptop. "How's things?" Gertrude says.

"Yeah, hanging in there."

"Good to hear, Maxwell. So I just want to introduce Percy, a colleague of mine in HR, who will just be sitting in with me today."

Percy? Not a name you come across every day. "Hello Maxwell," Percy says. He finally looks up and offers his hand. He need not have bothered though. It is the limpest handshake I have ever had. Really quite offensive.

"Hi," I nod in Percy's general direction whilst he gives me his pathetic hand.

"So obviously this is the appraisal. We have your completed appraisal form, thanks for sending that through."

Percy is just looking at his laptop.

"I just wanted to go through some of the Key Performance Indicators that we use, so you understand the matrix you are judged against."

This is all getting a bit serious.

"And just looking at your figures against these, there is a little bit of a downward curve over the last eighteen to twenty-two months."

Downward curve?

"I must admit I wasn't aware of that. I thought my billing was on track. I appreciate my debt levels might be a bit higher than I would have liked. But I can't always control that, as you know."

"No, I do appreciate that, Maxwell. But as part of the appraisals this year there is a strong focus at managerial level on the KPIs, so if we need to help staff increase their performance around these, then we need that feedback. But we also need to make clear what those KPIs are in the first place, just so there is no ambiguity around that, and to make sure that any underperformance against those is not as a result of that misunderstanding. That's part of our job."

Underperformance? I cast the occasional glance at Percy. He still isn't looking at me. Probably too embarrassed after that ridiculous handshake he offered earlier. I don't blame him. I wouldn't be able to keep eye contact either if I had delivered something as limp as that.

Leaving the appraisal and feeling a bit miffed, if I am honest. What was all that about? Cutting through the HR waffle, the upshot is basically 'pull your office socks up'. Bit more downbeat than any of my previous sixteen appraisals. Must just be some office-wide push to increase performance across the board. Yes, that's what it is. It won't be just me. I expect this will be general stuff for everyone. They could have just sent us all a firm-wide e-mail and saved us all the bother.

13

Office Cards

Today in the office I have done very little, in fact fuck all really. I am only just actually getting round to one of the first jobs I do on any given day. Purging my overnight e-mails. Each day the new unread e-mails pop up with blue highlighting. They load up and ping on screen. Sometimes the whole screen is a sea of blue. The first job is to sift through and separate the important, relevant e-mails from the spam ones. The spam needs to be identified and purged.

So locate these vicious little bastards and then whittle them down. But they aren't always that easy to identify. They like to masquerade as productive, relevant e-mails. I have become more adept at identifying them over the years. Then right click and delete them without giving them the satisfaction of reading them. So, these are all straight into the recycle bin and then a nice Ctrl and A and delete all. It is the computer form of colonic irrigation. Worse than even the spam e-mails, though, are the potential viruses. Spam is annoying, and a massive collective drain on office worker productivity, but is ultimately harmless. Viruses are potentially career- ending. Most office workers who have clicked on these have in the end been shown the door at this place. And the ones who haven't realise in the fullness of time that the stigma and shame of clicking a virus e-mail that infects the whole firm never quite leaves you.

It is getting easier to fall into the hacker's traps as well. Lapses in concentration and hangovers on a Monday morning increase your chances of falling victim to an e-mail virus. You have to stay vigilant. These e-mails are designed to look legitimate. But they are Trojan Horses. As soon as you click them it will start pinging porn or something worse to every other office worker.

And then there are the birthday e-mails. Birthdays in an office environment are very different from birthdays on civvy street. In most other working environments, if it is your birthday, one of your mates will probably offer to buy you a pint or two and a packet of peanuts down the pub at the end of the day. But the convention in offices the length and breadth of the country is that the office worker whose birthday it is, will send an e-mail round to everyone in the firm to announce that it is their birthday and – crucially – that cakes have been bought for everyone in their team, department or floor. That means a good chunk of their pay packet that month being swallowed up by caramel doughnuts.

Then there are the leavers' e-mails. Leavers' e-mails are always a bit odd. Often there is a short e-mail from the relevant office about the person's impending departure. I have a quick scan of my e-mails this morning. There is bound to be one. There is one. Sent 8.58am.

Dear all,

It has been such a pleasure working here for the last sixteen months. I have loved working with you all and made some friends for life. I feel like I have grown as a person and in my career and will take this with me as a platform onwards and upwards. Please do keep in touch and I will see you all soon hopefully.

Lots of love, Stacy

I have no idea who Stacy is, but I am glad that she views me in such glowing terms. A leaver also means another leaving collection is imminent. This time for Stacy. Whoever she is. These cards are accompanied by a money collection and card-signing exercise. The money is usually requested as a deposit directly into someone's bank account, usually the office worker tasked with sorting out a leaving present. Out of the office workers in this building, there are probably only about sixteen I know. So invariably I'll be signing a card for an office worker that I've never even spoken to or had e-mail traffic with. It is like signing a leaving card passed round on a bus from one of the passengers in honor of a passenger just about to get off.

Recently there has been a spate of leavers. I'm not quite sure why. Anyway, whatever the reason, the sheer volume of these leaving cards that have entered into circulation means a good proportion of the working day is allocated to signing sessions. Sometimes it is just a conveyor belt of cards being passed around. I've got a bit lazy over the years with the messages in these cards. The funniest messages are usually those from Management: 'Best of luck for the future' or 'You will be missed' or 'Come back soon', that kind of thing. Seriously. The same people that sacked them in the first place...

14

Tony the Office Cyclist

Today I am at my desk fairly early. Clive still isn't back. Daniel isn't in yet, which is always good. Clare is back from Magaluf though. Apparently she went raving every night. She is on the phone with Sean from IT, probably having similar issues as I had a couple of weeks ago.

It is around 8.45am, and I am unusually in the office earlier this morning. Not sure why. Maybe got a lucky break with my facial hair. I am not often in the office this early nowadays, but when I am this is usually about the time that Tony – the office cyclist – arrives. I am happy to admit I don't know anything about cycling, apart from when I used to BMX around my house when we were growing up. He sits just a few banks away from me. I went to his thirtieth birthday party a few years ago. I think he cycled to that also. And back, probably drunk.

Tony, like many office cyclists, likes to walk into the office in full-on cycle gear and with his bike in tow. He even takes his bike into the office lifts with him. Tony tends to like to wear quite a lot of Lycra. I would be a little self-conscious if I wondered about the office in bright yellow lycra, but Tony is at one with it. Really tight lycra to boot. Really bright, fluorescent or neon coloured lycra. A whole rainbow of lycra colours. Bright yellow in the office really stands out amongst the general brown. The other notable feature about Tony is his legs. They are massive, the way cyclists legs often are.

There is also a certain hum in the air when Tony walks in. A waft of *eau de l'homme.* Not a perfume that has been carefully and painstakingly put together in a laboratory. No, this odour is made from miles and miles of human sweat, forged into the Lycra and then allowed to incubate for fifteen to twenty minutes. It is then tested on anyone already in the office at this time as Tony strides through the floor like a deformed catwalk model. I'm not sure whether Tony is aware of the effect this stench has on other people. He probably can't smell it himself. He usually heads over and stops for a chat before hitting the office showers. Clare, probably aware of what is coming, heads to the toilet.

"Morning Max, how are you."

"Yeah ok Tony, although if I had known you would be wearing that shade of yellow today I would have brought my sunglasses with me."

Tony laughs. Just then Daniel arrives in a fluster. "Nearly lost it with this idiot on the bus this morning" Daniel says.

"Oh good morning Daniel" I say.

"Real fucking idiot. Was on his phone the whole journey. Just talking shit. And he smelt really bad. I mean what day is it? Monday? Yes it's Monday so he has had the whole weekend to shower you would think wouldn't you. But no. Not this guy. Dirty bastard."

I am laughing so hard inwardly.

"Sorry, Tony, you were saying something before Daniel rudely interrupted you. How was your bike ride to work this morning?"

"It was a good run this morning Max. Made it this morning in thirty-six minutes," Tony says as he stands over me, navel fully on show and at about my eye level, beneath the outrageous shrunken yellow lycra. To be fair, whether or not this is a personal best for Tony is not currently top of my mind in importance.

"There were the usual few pricks on the road today though. Probably lost five minutes, maybe more, 'cause of that, but, all in all, generally happy with my time."

"You getting grief from motor car users again, Tony?" I ask.

"Yeah, just the usual though really. Giving all the chat out the window about how we should be off the road because we don't pay road tax. That kind of thing. A few older folk who have no spatial awareness and probably shouldn't still be driving. I am pretty immune to it all now."

"Hey, Tony," Daniel says, forcing himself into the conversation after his tirade a few seconds ago. "Do you reckon I can ride pillion with you some day?"

"Daniel, I would be delighted. Bring your helmet and goggles." Tony laughs loudly.

"Goggles? How fast do you go? I will see if I can find my old chemistry goggles from school," Daniel says.

Just as Tony is taking his gloves off, a small globule of sweat cannons off his hand and lands right on my desk. I don't think he notices.

"Tony, I don't know why you don't just get on the train like everyone else," Daniel says. "Way too much exercise in the morning. You will have a heart attack before lunch."

"Daniel, it is you, my friend, who will be entering the cemetery prematurely. Where's your daily exercise? A couple of trips to the printer every day?" Tony replies.

"So where is Clive, by the way?" Tony asks. "I haven't seen him in the office for the last week or so."

"On jury service," says Daniel.

"Eh. Jury service?" I say to Daniel. "I thought he had a chest infection."

"Clive isn't capable of getting chest infections, Maxwell. His lungs are too posh for that," Daniel says.

"You could have told me, Daniel. I mean, he only sits next to me," I say, annoyed.

"You didn't ask, Maxwell."

"Jury service, eh?" says Tony. "I did that once a long time ago. I think it was a highly complicated white-collar fraud case."

"Did it involve Daniel nicking that fiver out my desk drawer that time?" I say.

Tony laughs. "I don't think you would need a jury for that one, Maxwell."

"Charming, that is, Maxwell," Daniel says. "Anyway, I wonder what crime Clive has got. I can imagine him in a jury actually. He will be in his element there. He has probably bought one of those judge's wigs. Holding court in court. I can see it now," I say.

"Not sure he is representative of a typical man on the street though," says Tony.

"I applied for jury service once," Daniel says.

"You don't apply for jury service, Daniel. They ask you. Pick you at random," I say.

"So how do they know I am not on holiday that week?" Daniel says.

"They don't. But it's compulsory. So in that sense they don't give a shit if you are on holiday."

"What if a douse myself in alcohol and pretend I am an alcoholic?"

"I wouldn't worry too much Daniel. I don't think they will calling you up for jury service in the very near future" I say.

Tony laughs.

"Anyway, see you in a bit. Duty calls. I have a new starter to mentor later," Tony says and with that, he is off in a final flash of luminous Lycra. My eyes might take a little while to settle back down.

15

The Post Room Incident

Today in the office I need to do a piece of large-scale photocopying. There are photocopiers on every floor in the office. At any one time, you are usually not more than ten feet away from a copier. Someone, somewhere, in the office is on a photocopier at almost every time of the working day. The queues for the photocopier are sometimes massive. But the basic copiers can only handle A4 and A3. Anything larger than that requires the copiers in the post room. The post room houses all the heavy-duty office machines. Large-scale printing, large-scale cutting, and resizing machines. It is like some kind of torture chamber.

Only post room staff are qualified to operate this machinery. Entering the post room is like entering into a different world. It is like stepping out of the office. It is like having a car garage in the middle of the office. The banter is different. They aren't constrained by the etiquette of the office. They aren't bound by the same rules. The radio is always on. There are no politics. There is no risk of anything getting back to Management. The post room staff have been reduced over the years to a select few though. Part of general cost-cutting. Reduction of overheads. Outsourcing. Going to a paperless environment.

The post room is a short walk around and down some corridors. As I draw closer I can hear the sound of slightly raised voices. This is nothing particularly unusual. These guys don't adhere to the official rules anyway. Probably just the usual blokey banter. But today there is even more than usual; there is what I can only describe as some form of high-pitched wailing.

"Howard, pull me back, pull me back!" comes a familiar but panic-stricken voice. What is going on? I open the door. I see Tim, a post room trainee, bending over one of the heavy-duty guillotine machines. Howard, the senior office worker and boss of the post room, has his arms around Tim's waist. At first, I think Howard is administering the Heimlich manoeuvre on Tim to dislodge some food stuck in Tim's throat. But on a closer look, it looks as though Tim's tie has got caught in the guillotine machine and it's steadily sucking him in. Howard is trying to free Tim using brute force but this is only making matters worse as each time he pulls Tim, his tie seems to be tightening (not to mention the fact that he will soon be sustaining serious rib injuries). Tim is screaming – I think for his Mum. I have to do something. One option is to get hold of Howard from the rear and try to pull both Howard and Tim back. No, that won't work. I won't get around Howard's waist. He is a big boned lad. The better option is to attempt to loosen Tim's tie, or, failing that, hold Tim's hand in his last moments.

Tim's face seems to have the same sense of anguish on it as my wife's had when she was in labour with my

71

daughter. That same look of 'do something immediately to alleviate my pain otherwise I will headbutt you in the face. And put that fucking bottle of wine down aswell.'

I still remember the moment like it was yesterday. It's incredible that something so perfect (in the case of my daughter and not anything Tim might currently produce) can be created from such brutality.

But I am not in the labour ward and I need to do something. Adrenaline kicks in. I drop my paper plan and quickly begin to loosen Tim's tie.

This is a labour of love for me. As you would expect I much prefer taking ties off to putting them on. The knot is really tight. He must have mastered the art. But I go at it. After a brief struggle it eventually comes loose. Tim falls back. His face is white as a sheet. He is gasping for air. He is stuttering something incoherent.

"Why the hell are you wearing a tie anyway?" Howard shouts. "I fucking told you last time you wore a tie. What do you need a tie for anyway? Does it help you to print or photocopy? No, it doesn't. Do you wanna be like those tossers out there?" Howard carries on, gesticulating towards the rest of the office. "That's the last time I save your skin if you wear that streak of piss around your neck again."

The lecture from Howard seems to be over. Tim is still a shambles on the floor though.

Howard turns to me and, as if the incident hasn't happened. He is immediately back to his usual friendly self.

"Maxwell, my boy, what can we do for you?" he asks, calmly as you like. Howard served in the military.

And not in the same way as some young scally who has done three weekends in the Territorial Army and thinks he was in the Paras. I think Howard has genuinely been shot a few times. That is probably why he can switch from a crisis to tranquil calmness at the flick of a switch. It also means he is not a man to be trifled or interfered with in any sense of the word.

"Yeah, sorry to trouble you, Howard, but I need a large one doing," I say. There is no need to elaborate. Howard and the post room lads seem OK with me. The rest of the staff have to sign a form to log something into the print room. They never ask me though.

"No problem, leave it on the pile, son. Tim will deal with it for you when he is finished on the toilet," Howard jokes in Tim's direction. Tim is still a shambles on the floor.

"Just a thought," I unwisely say, "but shouldn't you be logging this incident down in the office health and safety incident file?"

I am, quite incredibly, one of the office first aiders. I get an additional £22 a month for being a nominated first aider, and apart from the money, believe it or not, I take my responsibilities seriously. I took a three hour first aid course a few years ago, which involved trying to resuscitate some plastic dummies in the office, and that has qualified me as a fully fledged first aider. There are full mugshots of me up in the communal areas of the office with a St John's Ambulance sticker next to them. The unwelcome consequence of this is that every time someone breaks a nail, they feel the need to report it to me by sending an e-mail. Some are in jest, some are serious. Howard, though, is no fan of health and safety legislation. He is old school in that way. Management has put a health and safety poster up in the print room containing the ten health and safety commandments. Howard has covered this up with a dartboard. He comes from an era where people didn't have to sign a form to go up a ladder, generally didn't wear helmets unless they were at war, and only wore protective goggles if they were snorkeling on holiday.

"I assume you are joking?" Howard says. "What am I going to write? That this numpty," he says, pointing again at Tim, who is still on the floor, "decides it is a good idea to wear ties whilst using one of my machines? Is that what you are getting at? They can kiss my ass."

"Don't worry. I've captured it in high definition and will be posting it on YouTube later. Reckon it'll be viral by midnight!" I reply. "We might be able to make some money out of this, Howard. Tell you what. You can take forty percent."

"Now you're talking my language. Did you get my best side though?" Howard says.

"Only an ass shot, I'm afraid! Quite a different website if you want me to post that," I reply.

16

The Stationary Cupboard

I am in the coffee shop, supping on my usual coffee, just served up by Noah. Noah himself is out back, doing some kind of stocktake.

There is no one in the coffee house today. I mean absolutely no one. Not even Jam and toast man. Not even him.

Noah comes over, and sits down on the table.

"Is it something you said? Or do you need to change your aftershave, my friend?" he says, pointing to all the empty seats.

"Yeah, why is it so quiet today then?" I ask. "Dunno, Maxwell, but I will take it. I've been rushed off my feet the last few days."

"Anyway, you will be glad to know that I paid privately for an MRI scan after my coffee house fall. Still waiting for the results" I say.

"Oh good, good. Did they find your brain then?"
"So yeah, I think they found it lurking in the left- hand corner." Noah laughs.

"What you up to at the weekend Maxwell?"

"Not really thought about it yet. I don't ever really tend to until I get to the weekend. What I will do though, Noah, and what weekends are for, is to lie in until at least 12.36pm."

"There is a lot of the student in you still then, Maxwell."

"Well, I still try to get into the cinema on my old student NUS card, if that's what you mean."

"Yeah, the nose hair won't help you on that front, Max. Eighteen-year-olds generally don't have clumps of nose hair."

"Anyway explain this to me. How come Monday to Friday, the whole world needs to be at work for 9am. Why 9am? 10am would be much more civilised."

"9am? My day starts at 6am, Maxwell."

"Yeah but you knock off at 2pm, Noah."

A customer comes in. Noah goes to serve him coffee to go that comes from, he says, somewhere in the Madagascan hills, and then comes back and sits down.

"Tell me, Noah. And be honest with me," I say. "Always honest, my friend."

"That coffee you just served that customer, is it really from the Madagascan hills? Or is it just from a big jar from Lidl?"

Noah laughs. "I cant tell you the secrets of this place Maxwell. You gotta keep people guessing."

"Can I be Frank with you Max?"

"You can be whoever you want to be with me Noah, we have known each other long enough."

"Ok so don't take this the wrong way, but its your face."

"What about my face?"

"Did you shave this morning?"

"Yes. I shave pretty much most days Noah, apart from on the weekend. I have quite rapid facial hair growth, as you well know. Why do you ask?"

"So what's going on with these bits?" he says, pointing to some bits on my face. How are you going to impress if you keep turning up to the office looking like a wino?"

"Thanks for that, Noah. I wouldn't have known until tonight."

"He who isn't honest with others, can't be honest with himself."

"How about this one: he who points out other people's facial hair is likely to get a slap round the chops. Now let me get to the office. You can carry on pretending to be busy."

3.30pm

Later the same day I am sat at my desk and since Noah has made me self-conscious about my face, I have been keeping a bit of a low profile. Getting some admin done. A bit of stocktaking. In particular, I am running low on stationery. I need some pencils, staples and ring binders. There is an office procedure for ordering stationery, like there is an office procedure for pretty much everything, even though the stationery cupboard is about ten yards away from me. But I am currently out of staples and shit so I need to put a formal request in. I can't just grab what I need. A request needs to be made to the stationery monitor office worker. This request cannot be made with just a simple e-mail either. There is a form to fill in. The form then needs to be countersigned by another office worker. That form is then scanned in and dispatched to the stationery section of the administration team. At the last count, the administration team comprised in the region of, I think, thirty-eight different sections.

Once you have located the stationery team from the dropdown section of the administration section, you are finally in a position to send the e-mail request. Immediately comes the auto-response e-mail: 'Thank you for your e-mail. We aim to deal with all enquiries and requests just as soon as possible, and no later than four working days from receipt.'

The average response time is in the region of four days. Four fucking days to get my hands on some staples not more than ten yards away from me.

17

Do You Look Like My Husband?

I strongly believe I have a medical condition. I call it restless office worker syndrome. It may not be medically recognised. But that doesn't mean I don't have it.

I think I may have always had it at low levels. I get a bit more restless when my stress levels are high. Put simply, the main symptom is an inability to stay in one place, mentally or physically, for longer than about twenty minutes. I just need to move. Not in a John Travolta way. Not in that way. I just need to stay on the move. This is not actually very helpful for an office worker who should be sat at his screen from 9am–1pm and then again from 2–5pm. So, as the time is 9.20am and I am therefore twenty minutes into the working day, I need a break.

In the office, my outlet for restless office syndrome is trips to the office kitchen and making loads of hot drinks. On my last count, I think I averaged about fifteen cups a day. Around eleven of these I probably didn't want. Office convention is generally that people tend to take it in turns to do rounds for each other on each bank of 4. On my bank of desks, though, it is every woman and man for themselves. There is one major reason for this: there is no way in this world that I will be drinking anything that Daniel might produce. Clare also won't have Daniel make a drink, since the last time he put milk in her green tea. Clive is a bit too suave to make anyone else drinks.

There are several kitchen areas dotted around the office serving various departments. Our department's kitchen is a short walk from my desk. There is a small fridge in the kitchen. I often like to have a little rootle and tootle around in the fridge. The fridge is in the kind of condition you might expect from a fridge used by hundreds of office workers. Some of the more industrious office workers store their high-protein vegan salad in the fridge, in little recycled plastic containers, with their names written in black markers on the top – 'Sarah – Accounts', by way of example. And there is always a bottle of champagne. I've never known why. But it is always there.

One of the cupboards, along with probably a smidgen of E. coli at the back, houses a huge selection of cups and mugs. Over the years I have worked out that coffee mugs fall into one of five different categories.

Mug type 1. The generic mug. These are communal, to be used by everyone. They are identified usually by being nondescript. They are usually one colour, often a dull colour. White or beige. Possibly brown.

Mug type 2. The garden centre mugs. These are not intended to be communal. They belong to individual office workers. These mugs are readily identifiable as such. They are identified by people's names, much like the labels on the items in the fridge. They aren't highly creative. So, there are plenty of mugs in the cupboard with the name Dave or Sarah. These are usually bought from garden centres, or whilst on holiday in Margate.

Mug type 3. The emotional mugs. These also belong to individual office workers. But they are not as obvious as the Dave or Sarah mugs. They are identified by some form of emotional or meaningful print or artwork attached to the mug. It could be a famous world landmark that means a lot to that particular office worker. But equally, it could be a person. An example of this is one of the mugs that has a photo of a baby. Some office workers have taken a picture of their little one and superimposed it on a cup.

Mug type 4. The joke mugs. These fall somewhere into a grey area. Not completely communal, but not necessarily belonging to anyone either. They are the joke mugs. Every office has one. You have to be careful with these. Some of them have their little messages just on one side, so these could be assumed to be a category 1 mug, just plain white or beige. But on the other side, you could be the office perv or office knobhead or whatever.

I used to have a mug. It probably fell into mug type 4. It was a mug with pictures of mould all over it. The cleaners kept trying to wash it off. I lost it a few weeks back. So I have been using the category 1 mugs since.

Today I have what I think is a category 1 mug. I have my drink in hand and am enroute back to my desk – a black coffee (two spoons of coffee this morning to try to wake me up), which is my normal as I don't really trust the milk in the office fridge.

Suddenly there is a scream from behind me. A real shriek.

"Hey, that's my mug!"

This is another problem with the open-plan office. Everyone around you will hear an argument. And you know that everyone is listening to the argument. Everyone has stopped working in unison just to tune in to the argument. I know the voice. It belongs to a fellow office worker who took a dislike to me from the start. We previously clashed about a year ago, and since then, I think she views me as a bit of a dickhead. I double-check the mug. Oh shit. The other side is a picture of her on her wedding day. Bride and groom. One of the most personal mugs you could have. This is not going to go well. She comes steaming over to me.

"Er… oh, sorry. I had no idea this was your cup. I just assumed it was one of the office mugs."

"How ridiculous!" she replies, her voice seething with contempt like I have just murdered her entire family. "Look at the picture. That's my husband on our wedding day. Does he look like you?"

I take a look. No, he doesn't actually. Thank fuck for that at the very least.

18

The Men's Toilet

The office's men's toilets are in fact quite pleasant inside. Not that they in the same league as the toilets in a five-star London hotel. They don't have a man stationed in them selling sweets. But I have occasionally seen cleaners in there with a mop and bucket, and there is a hamper at the side of one of the sinks that has something called potpourri in it, which as I understand it is an attempt to make the toilet smell fragrant.

However, I do have a problem with the handwash in the toilet. Management has recently been on a drive to cut costs. That drive on costs causes a few redundancies here and there, depleted levels of stationery around the office, no complimentary biscuits in the office, and so on and so forth.

But cost-cutting on handwash in the toilet is a step too far in my world. They're essentially watering the handwash down. The effect of this is that even the slightest pressure on the handwash drop-down mechanism means a jet of handwash coming out much faster than expected. This often means the liquid hitting not just the hands but also spraying the groin. That also means someone from Management actually had the handwash as an agenda point at a meeting – and, even worse, that means other members of management voting in favour of watering down the handwash. Apart from the fact that by watering the handwash down they are stripping it of its primary purpose, which is to clean, it also means a piss patch on my suit trousers. Black suits might absorb this. But grey suits don't. And that, in turn, means standing on a chair and lining my watery groin up with the hand dryer in the gents'. That is never a good look when other people come in.

19

The Sweet Shop

Today has been a really long day in the office. The office has been noisy. Clare even lost her temper with a customer. Probably missing the party season in Magaluf and taking it out on customers. Some office workers on a bank of four further down the floor seem to be talking about the weather and comparing prices of package holidays.

Daniel has his left hand down his crotch. I am sure that it is purely platonic and non-sexual, but who knows with Daniel.

The computer is on but I am just staring at it. I have switched off today. This would be a good moment to be sat on Lennox's sofa. A moment of reflection, contemplation.

I think back to my youth. Growing up, I used to have a job in the local sweet shop. About fifteen, I think I was. My dad had strongly suggested I needed a job, and even though I was probably always destined for office work, I was just a little too young to be working in an office at fifteen years of age. The local sweet shop was stacked full of jars of sweets of every type and colour you could imagine. The thing about sweet shops is that everyone is happy in a sweet shop – staff and customers alike. The colours. The smells. Just confectionery and sugar everywhere. Pretty much the opposite of the office. No brown in site. And probably because of that you could pretty much charge what you wanted for sweets. Almost anything else in any other shop people would question the price of, argue you down, barter with you. But not in a sweet shop. People pay anything for sweets. You could double the price and people would still not bat an eyelid. I know. I used to do it.

Still, you do still need a bit of bravado to work in a sweet shop at fifteen. I was... well, probably a bit of a cocky little twat if I am honest. The manager of the shop showed me how to operate the till, which back in those days, of course, was all mechanical, not computerised. He showed me how to do basic accounts and check my takings at the end of the day. But perhaps most importantly of all, he showed me how to serve the customers. *This business is all about people, he used to say, it isn't the money or even the sweets. It is the people.* If you could get on with the people that passed through the door then it was easy for them to part with their cash. Literally like taking candy from a baby (or giving them candy in this context).

It was a usual Saturday morning in the sweet shop. I had my head down and buried in one of my comics, and with my baseball cap on the wrong way round. The bell on the front door rang. As I looked up, I saw three girls walk into the shop babbling away. Oh shit, a group of girls together. And they were from my year at school, to make it worse. I was fumbling about like any teenager would with girls from their school walking into their shop. I could talk to anyone, even at that age – old folk, businessmen, chancers, small gangs of youths, gypsies. Anyone. Except three girls from my school. I may have been dribbling slightly.

They were all whispering to each other, looking around the shop but occasionally glancing over and giggling. I was trying to hide behind my baseball cap, having flipped it round the right way. They had recognised me from school. I could feel the blood rushing to my head already. There was no escape. When you're serving in a shop, you can't just nip off to the toilet for a comfort break when there are customers in the shop. Usually I wanted sales, but quite frankly, just for that moment, I would have been more than happy if they had just left the shop.

As was probably always going to be the way, they all approached the counter. "Hiya, you," the tallest of the group said. "You go to our school, don't you?" she carried on with an air of confidence. "You are mates with Wendy, aren't you?"

Too many questions in quick succession.

I was trying to tell myself to act cool, of course. Calm yourself Maxwell. Remind yourself of who you are. This is your shop. Your manor. You call the shots in this joint. I started chewing as if I had some gum. I didn't.

"Err yeah, that's right. Fifth year, you lot are in, aren't you?" I said without any swagger or confidence whatsoever.

"Wot you working here for?" the tall girl said whilst throwing her hair back and twirling it at the same time.

"Just been working here for the past few months. Get some money in," I replied. Yes that's it Maxwell. That will impress them. Make out you are a man of means. Even at fifteen.

"Seems like a waste of a Saturday morning, if you ask me," she scoffed.

"Stop teasing him, Karen," one of the other girls said. I was a bit taken aback. I didn't expect that. She seemed genuine. She had thick, long blonde hair, and the greenest of eyes. Just piercing green eyes.

"Ignore them," she said. "I think it is brilliant. Hi, my name is Mandy."

That was one of those moments. I was still focused on this girl called Mandy. Just Mandy.

As she got to the door she glanced back and smiled. "Just one thing, though," she said.

"Err... yes?" I mumbled.

"You haven't actually got any gum in your mouth, have you?" She winked and left.

My mouth remained open for about ten minutes. Ten years later we were married...

4.36pm

Back to today I have just eaten an apple that I brought into work with me. It has been in my pocket all day but I have just rinsed it well in the kitchen. I don't have a bin though. No one does anymore. Some time ago, I think probably at the same time that management decided to implement a clean environment policy, they introduced a sister policy that had the effect of removing everyone's bin. Previously, we all had bins at our desks. Nothing grandiose. Just small round bins. How times have changed though. With the advent of recycling, the bins were removed. These have been replaced on each floor with colour-coded bins in each floor's kitchen. You know each colour corresponds with a type of waste. Bottles are green, food is brown, etc. Each bin has a tick for items that you could chuck into that bin, and a big cross representing the 'contaminative' items. The list of contaminative items is a bit over the top. One of the bins suggests that rucksacks are a prohibited item. Of course they are. Who in their right mind would bring a rucksack into work and then throw it into the food bin? I do my bit for the planet and put my discarded apple core in the correctly coloured food waste bin.

20

The Office Fire Drill

Today the fire alarm has just gone off. There are often tests. But this one is going on too long for a test. This means one of two things. Either someone in the building has burnt their toast and there is a real fire somewhere in the building, or much more likely is that this is the bi-annual fire drill. I have never understood the biannual fire drill. I get the weekly testing of the alarm. The weekly testing is for a short period and is usually the same time each week. Just testing that the ringer dinger and the battery in the smoke alarms are working. I get all that.

But the biannual office fire drill I don't get. I assume the concept is to test everyone's sense of urgency, how they respond in an emergency. But most of the time when the fire alarm goes off, unless your eyes are burning in plumes of smoke, pretty much everyone assumes this is just a drill. And that really takes the sting out of it. So the sense of urgency is just not really there.

The only office workers who react to the fire drill with anything other than complete and total apathy are the 'designated' fire wardens scattered around the office. This is their time to shine, to come out from the shadows of obscurity. The fire wardens are, on the face of it, just normal office workers. But they've volunteered for the role of fire warden. Volunteering to be a fire warden needs no formal training. Not like me being one of the office first aiders and all that. All they seem to do is put on their high-vis yellow jacket with 'Fire Marshal' written on the back when the fire alarm goes off, take out a clipboard and point people in the direction of the doors.

Each floor also has its own designated fire warden. Our floor fire warden is… how can I put this politely… very much not an athlete. She has worked in the company for at least sixty-five years. No one quite knows exactly how old she is, but she must not be far off getting a telegram from the queen. Her role is to usher us us all to the fire exits, like a shepherd herding sheep. She doesn't lead by example though. Her own response time for informing her office co- workers that this is the annual fire drill is about two and a half minutes. At least one and a half minutes of that is locating and then putting on her high-vis yellow jacket. If she is setting the example of how to react in the event of a fire for others to follow, there would be many, many more people hospitalised in the event of a real fire.

The fire alarm is also loud. Really loud. I mean, I am not especially old. I used to play the drums. I am used to loud noise. But whoever programmed these fire alarms must have some shares in a hearing aid company or something. It is like a thousand dogs on steroids all barking at the same time. It sounds like nothing else.

Babies screaming, white noise, fingernails down a blackboard. It is worse than all of them. And you can't run to get away from the noise. You must always walk. I'm fucked if I am walking if there is ever a real fire. I will be off like Usain Bolt on speed.

"This is a fire drill. Please move quickly to your nearest exit!" our floor fire warden shouts after about ten minutes. I have heard this speech before. Twice a year. About twenty times in my lifetime in this place. She is still reading off a clipboard though. How can she possibly not remember the words?

"Do not take any personal belongings," she carries on bellowing, her voice starting to crack with either age or pride. "Move quickly and with conviction to the stairs. Do NOT stop to help anyone else out."

Does that mean that if Jim from Accounts tripped and fell in front of me, I would have to trample over him like someone completely devoid of any kind of moral compass? I mean, Jim from Accounts may go on a bit, but that doesn't mean I will be leaving him to die in a fire. In my world, and despite our differences, we still look out for our brethren in the office worker community.

The drill commences. No sense of urgency obviously. By now the fire would've engulfed the building and everyone in it. Luckily, this is just a rehearsal. Still, could be worse. You could be on the toilet.

As pretty much the whole of the building emerges at street level, the usual carnage ensues. The entrance and exit from the building are directly onto the main road, and there are a lot of people in this building.

There is no actual area to gather into. So, people end up spilling into the road. People in cars honk their horns like they sometimes do when they pass a load of office workers in unsuitable clothing standing on the side of the road in winter. The next step is the register. This is the only time in anyone's office life that you have to answer to your name being read out. It is like going back to school assembly. Adults shouldn't have to shout out their names in alphabetical fashion under any circumstances. It is demeaning. It is even more demeaning that this register is being carried out on the street as other people are walking by.

"Once we have called your name out and you have confirmed your presence, you may return to your workstations."

I am relatively early in the alphabet, being an "O", but as I shout a slightly sarcastic "Here!" when my name is called, I look back at Xavier from the third floor. Poor sod.

A few minutes later and I am back at my desk. There is an e-mail from the senior fire warden. It reads:

All, just to inform you the annual fire assessment training that was instigated at 11.31am was completed by 11.46. The initial evacuation response time [I think that means the time to leave the building] was timed at two minutes forty-eight seconds. This is an improvement of twenty seconds to our last assessment and thanks go to the diligence and hard work of all the volunteer fire wardens.

The response times may have improved, but there is probably at least one office worker in A and E having been clipped by a car, two or three on a drip in intensive care with hypothermia, and a large proportion with untreatable tinnitus.

21

Shaving in an energy crisis

Today I got the earlier 7.45am commuter train to town, not my usual 8.08. It arrived at the station at 8am, so just 15 minutes late, which historically is not too bad. So I have more time in the coffee house which is where I am currently talking to Noah.

"Money, Maxwell, money. Whoever said money doesn't solve a problem didn't have enough to solve it," Noah is saying. That isn't really a Noah comment. He is clearly slightly agitated today. It isn't like him. He must be hanging around me too much.

"You OK, Noah?" I ask with some genuine concern.

"Yeah, just getting fleeced by my energy supplier. My gas and electric bills are going through the roof."

"I know. Mine too."

"Eh? You are a tenant."

"Yeah but I still have to pay Wendy for what I use."

"Surely she gives you mate's rates? And anyway, Max, and don't take this the wrong way, but I would imagine you live in quite a bit of darkness."

"Nothing wrong with being frugal, Noah. There is an energy crisis round the corner, you know."

"Yeah. But please tell me you have the lights on

when you are in the toilet? Actually, I get it now!" Noah starts laughing quite uncontrollably.

"What do you get, my friend?"

"That's why you always miss a bit when you are shaving. You shave in the dark. It is all starting to make sense now." Noah is still laughing. A proper belly laugh.

"No, I don't," I say. I have to think a bit though. "Yes you do. You do. So you get up, maybe around 6am, with your disposable razor in hand, just poised to start shaving. But then you wait until when Greenwich Mean Time daylight arrives so you can see what you are doing, because you, my good friend, are too tight to put the light on!"

I think this is the most I have ever seen Noah laugh.

Good job I have got thick skin.

"Anyway, talking of money, Noah, I was thinking about this the other day," I say.

"Go on?" Noah says, still laughing.

"Why does no one ever talk about how much they earn?"

"I am happy to tell you how much I don't earn, Maxwell," Noah laughs.

"No, I am being serious. So we talk about everything. You know that. But not how much we earn." Noah looks pensive. "Take my office, for example. No one ever talks out salary. And for good reason. There would probably be a mutiny. But Noah, and this is the thing here – people are happy to try to show other people how wealthy there are with a Ferrari or a £2000 pair of trainers. You know all the drippings of wealth."

"Don't like that word Max."

"What Ferrari?"

"No – drippings. Makes me feel a bit queasy."

"Anyway you get what I am saying."

"Maxwell, I would love to show you how rich I am. My Ferrari, though, is at the garage and my trainers are at the dry cleaners. But that said, Maxwell, on a serious note, you may have a point there. Maybe one for that book you have nowhere near started to right, what's it called again, oh yes *The Alien Jury.*"

"You aren't quite getting the idea of *The Alien Jury*, are you, Noah?"

"Not really, Maxwell. I like a book title to tell me what is in the book. Give me a clue. Light the way. Give me some direction, my friend."

"That surprises me, Noah. I thought you had a bit more imagination than that."

"Whatever book you write, I want you to completely throw me off the scent with the title on the front. I want it to be completely unrelated to its contents. If it is a book about music, I want the title to be something like... oh, I don't know... 'Improve your garden in five weeks'."

"Piss off, Noah, you are just being faeces now."

"Err, facetious, I think you mean, Maxwell."

"Yes, I know I did. That's what I said."

"Why don't you go pitch your book to our friend in the corner?" Noah gestures to the regular. The jam and toast man is in the house today.

"Yeah, I see your man is here again. Bless him. Two slices of jam and toast again, I assume?" I ask.

"How did you guess?"

97

"Anyway, got to get to the office. Its nearly nine. Can't be late. Just before I go though, you know your point on the book title."

"Yes."

"At least you remembered the name of the book didn't you?"

Noah is about to say something.

"No Noah don't say a word. Leave me with that small victory."

22

New Starters

Today, I'm in a contemplative mood in the office. I am not yet able mentally to get back into work mode. I am daydreaming a bit about content for *The Alien Jury,* but pleased that Noah remembered the title.

Somewhere on the far side of the office, I hear a new starter being introduced. This is a big office and there are many office workers in the building. There are therefore at any one time many disgruntled workers in this building. But the same is true of other companies across the land. So, as a result, office workers from different companies tend to swap over quite a bit. Like one big office revolving door. Hence new starters are born. There is little loyalty in big companies anymore. Office workers are just hired hands really.

"Morning, Kevin. This is Jane. She is just starting today in Accounts," I hear from somewhere on the other side of the floor. Poor Jane. She will be petrified. I can still remember the time I was shown around the floor as a new starter. The induction process is painful. You are delivered to your desk and asked to complete sixty-five different surveys. Equality and diversity. Health and safety. Manual handling. Fire assessment surveys.

The list is endless. Not pleasant. And all the while no one gives you the time of day. You have no clue where the toilets are, the kitchen, the stationery cupboard. Someone asks you to close a blind and you don't have a fucking clue how to operate it whilst everyone in the office just stares at you. Oh God, I just realised she is starting in Accounts. Her mentor will most likely be Jim. She will need a large wine tonight…

23

Spit and Sawdust

Today I am on the countdown to lunch. In more recent times and on particularly bad office days, getting to lunch is not too dissimilar to the feeling of seeing a Coca Cola sign in the desert. Some people stay at their desks over lunch. I don't get that. As an office worker, you are spending the best part of seven hours a day sitting on your arse. So, when the time arises when the government says you are legally entitled to a one- hour break, why would you want to continue to sit on your arse? But many of my fellow office workers do just that. I hope they are getting their five-a-day fruit and veg pieces and their seven to nine hours of sleep a night because they are failing badly in the exercise category. It wouldn't be so bad if the office cyclist sat through lunch. I am sure he is burning sufficient calories a day by going uphill in the wrong gear twice a day. But I just get the feeling that many of my other fellow office workers in this building who are rooted to their desks at lunch are more likely to be bingeing on five bags of crisps at night than doing some exercise in the evening after work.

Tuesday and Thursday are my gym days and today is a Tuesday. There are two gyms close to the office. One

101

is the big corporate gym that loads of office workers are members of. Staff discounts on memberships and all that. I went to the corporate gyms a couple of times when I first started in the office. Almost everyone in there is in Lycra. A different kind of Lycra outfit to Tony the cyclist though. Mainly designer Lycra. The kind of Lycra that YouTube lifestyle vloggers are vlogging about. Outfits that have some form of a self-cooling system built into their fabric. Outfits that need a hammer and chisel to get off. The corporate gym is big business. It is a mini fashion show. In the corporate gym, people apply their make-up *before* going for a workout. There are separate rooms where people are meditating and performing pilates or yoga. There are quiet rooms, adult rooms, rooms set up for flexible working. All of this isn't really for me. I don't want to work with other office workers and then work out with them also. An office worker needs some space.

So, I found this other little gym round the corner. Same kind of thinking, I suppose, as my niche, slightly backstreet coffee house. Still close enough to the office. All a bit spit and sawdust. The sign over the door is handwritten. It is a bit basic. There aren't state-of-the- art machines that work every part of your body or running machines that monitor your heart rate, blood pressure, cholesterol level and sperm count. No, with this gym, you get what you pay for, which is not really very much. But you aren't paying a small fortune in monthly subscriptions either. So that means a few dumbbells, a bit of rising damp, one running machine, and an army of blokes, most of whom who can't get their arms over their pecs. But I like this gym. This is probably also the only place that I am not at risk of bumping into Jim from Accounts.

1.10 pm

I have arrived at the gym and changed into my old PE kit from school. There is no designer Lycra going on here for me. Most of the punters here are larger blokes. There is a lot of grunting. And there is something called 'spotting' going on in this gym. That is basically when a couple of these fellas get together and decide to motivate others to lift heavy weights. The motivation isn't that subtle. It is when the motivator or 'grunter' grunts really loudly at the person lifting the weights (the gruntee), and about an inch from the gruntee's face. The first time I witnessed this I thought that the grunter was having some kind of medical problem and was concerned that no one around seemed to be doing anything about it. But the role of the grunter in this situation is to incentivise and adrenalise the gruntee, the idea being to elevate the gruntee to new heights and allow that one final repetition that either means the required weight is lifted or a load of ligaments is torn, whichever comes first. The sound of the grunter is usually really bad. The fact that it is considered acceptable by the other gym members is quite incredible. I live in constant fear of being collared by one of these chaps and asked to be a grunter for the day. So I stay aloof and never make eye contact.

I am halfway through the shoulder press when the man-mountain walks in. This chap is no ordinary gym bunny. In a gym full of wannabe bodybuilders, this fella is the big dog. He must be six foot ten and twenty stone of pure muscle. And he is well proportioned. Not like a lot of the others. Most of the others in here resemble Mr Incredible. You know, loads of muscle up top but they have been skipping on the leg days. The opposite of Tony the office cyclist. But not this guy. This guy has the legs to go with the arms. Everyone stops when he walks in. It is like he is a mini-celebrity. How the fuck did he get that big? No number of workouts, no amount of high-quality chicken, no protein powder would get you anywhere near his size. He should be in the circus or in the movies. He is bordering on a freak show.

Funny thing, though – when he speaks, he has the voice of a twelve-year-old girl. Appearances aren't everything.

1.36pm
After the gym I need some food. My body's metabolism can't handle what it could handle when I was in my twenties, so slowly I have been forced to move to healthier lunchtime options. There is probably too much choice for lunch now around the office. There are little delis, your chain food convenience, take-away outlets, little sandwich bars and, for the less discerning office worker, there is the late-night kebab house that is still just about open from the night before just round the corner.

The new food geared to the office worker, though, is avocado. It's everywhere at lunch. All the commercial sandwich shops, the health-conscious ones and the backstreet ones sell avocado. The only place you can't get avocado is the local kebab house, and I believe maybe McDonald's. I may be wrong on that front. Avocado is in every sandwich. Smashed avocado and tomato, avocado with eggs, avocado with ham, avocado with fucking everything. I think I have even once seen a smashed avocado with avocado sandwich.

Today I have ended up in the queue for a footlong at Subway. It is the school holidays. There are a load of kids, a load of kids with their parents, a couple of people who look like they are signing on, and a couple of fellow office workers. There are also some retired folk. The retired folk will add about fifteen minutes to the wait time. They seem to have forgotten the world of fast-paced commerce. Not even fast- paced – just normal-paced. They also tend to pay for everything with a mixture of 2p coins, 1p coins and vouchers. Not with their phone, or even a credit or debit card. And they never know what these amounts add up to. You would think they would work out how much their lunch costs and have the presence of mind to get their change ready before getting to the till. Occasionally they ask the servers to go through their purse or wallet to extract the right change. All very well-intentioned. But massively annoying when you are on a tight timeframe and you need to get back to the office and make some money for your company.

I contemplate going somewhere else. This queue looks like a fifteen-minuter.

Ahead of me, though, at the front of the queue I can hear someone going through their salad choices for their Subway.

"Any salads with your sandwich?" the Subway worker is asking.

"Ah yes, could I have everything apart from sweetcorn, tomato, peppers, olives, onions, cucumber, bacon sprinkles, gherkin and chilli."

There is a bit of silence. "So you just want lettuce then?" replies the bemused Subway worker.

"Yes, that's right... and a bit of garlic mayo sauce," the customer replies.

I head back to the office.

24

Felix

I hear a familiar voice at the end of the office – a distinctive and pompous voice. This is Felix. Felix Doberman. He will shortly be somewhere in the vicinity. Felix is the office greasy pole climber. Every office has one. The office worker that would do anything for progression up the greasy pole. Just talks shit to people all day. Usually non-consensual conversations, forced upon people who have done nothing to deserve it. Felix hardly ever does any actual work. Not that I do that much myself these days. But at least I am honest about it. And I have put in my pound of flesh to this place in the past. Not entirely sure Felix has.

But I am in the slightly unfortunate position of being underneath Felix (thankfully not physically), but from an office hierarchy perspective. The office operates as a tiered hierarchy. There is senior management. Then there is management. Then there are senior associates, associates and then junior associates. Then comes the assistants; they are split into about five categories. Then a few more layers under them. I forget what they are even though I must have been a member of each category at some point. Junior assistants, and then God knows what else. The office greasy pole climber is a senior associate. I am still an associate. I was knocked back for senior associate last year. I think the reason for my application was so that this man couldn't tell me what to do anymore. I was unsuccessful. So that gives him a measure of power over me. He enjoys exerting that power.

He likes the sound of his own voice, and he likes the look of his e-mails. He copies the whole world into every e-mail. No 'cc' list is big enough for him. He loves to send e-mails over a weekend to show how hard he works. Often you will find an email at 11.25 on a Sunday night in your Monday morning e-mails.

I do a quick scan of my recent e-mails. Oh, there we go. Four group emails timed at 12.06, 12.12, 12.22 and 12.37 from him – all of these to the whole office and all of them completely irrelevant.

He is getting closer. Here he comes.

"Maxwell, my boy," he says in his slightly absurd, put-on gentrified accent. He pretends to be from the landed gentry. He isn't.

"I have been pulled into a big meeting in London, and I need to be on a train in T minus two hours for a client meeting."

This isn't a conversation. This is a speech to the entire floor. He is completely aware of the fact that the whole of the office floor is listening to him. He wants an audience.

"So, I am going to have to ask you to cover for me in a meeting later on. Nothing too heavy. Just an induction speech to some of the new apprentices joining the office."

This is him demonstrating to the surrounding office workers that he is in control, that he can exert his authority at will. He is for some reason in charge of the training and mentoring of new apprentices. And given that he also fancies himself, I've never thought that to be a wise appointment.

"I think there will probably be about eight of them. I will e-mail their CVs to you in a moment if you need any prep time. Be doing me a big favour."

"Are you asking me or telling me?" I reply with sarcasm.

"Maxwell, don't be like that. No one else is around and capable of doing it."

"How do you know I can make it?"

"Checked your calendar on Outlook."

"I never gave you access to that! What are you doing snooping around my Outlook calendar? Isn't that some breach of data protection or my human rights?"

"Just general permission needed to access any associate's calendar. Anyway, let me know how it goes. We are looking to take an intake of no more than three for next year so could do with some feedback from an experienced associate. Anyway, got to fly now. Have to be at the London office by five. I will ping you an appointment through."

Knobhead.

25

Lack of Confidence at the Printer

I'm just starting the prep for this new starter presentation that Felix has forced on me. I don't need to do much prep for this presentation to be fair. I know it inside out. I was the office trainer in charge of newbies to the firm before Felix knew how to photocopy. The only thing I need to get my head around is who I am dealing with in this particular batch of new starters. Their backstory. Their life before the office. Everyone has a backstory. And that backstory is supposedly encapsulated in a two-page pitch for the job, at the same time serving as a potted summary of one's life and office career. The Curriculum Vitae. A very grand title for usually a pile of shit.

Who's in this pile then? I have eight to review. I need to allocate a couple of minutes for each. This can't be an in-depth review. It needs to be a cursory scan. But I have got adept at scanning through these CVs over the years. I need to look for the highlights.

There are never any photos attached to CVs. There used to be, but from around 2012, the photos just seemed to stop. I don't know the reason. I think it has to do with some legislation that has outlawed it. Whatever the reason, I miss the photos. A picture generally tells a thousand words, as the saying goes. Some of the pictures were hilarious. Full frontals. Airbrushed shots. Shots clearly from old passports. Photos from police line-ups. Action shots – holding a stapler, maybe operating a photocopier. Maybe adding photos makes it too much like a dating agency.

Company websites have people's faces splashed over them, usually in the 'meet the team' sections. Why not CVs anymore?

I need to print these CVs. Physically print them to a local printer near my desk. One day in the not-too-distant future, printers that print on paper will only be seen in museums, a bit like the typewriter. But just for the minute the printer is still being abused in the office.

Someone is hanging around the printer in front of me though. Looks to me like it might be Jane, the new starter from this morning. You can tell the new starters a mile off. They fumble with everything. All fingers and thumbs. Even though this printer looks like a spaceship, it is pretty simple to use. Switch on, log in and print the stored print job. Papers are spilling out all over the place. I feel sorry for her. I was a new starter once, full of the optimism of youth, ready to take on the corporate world. Not having a fucking clue.

"Hiya. Can I give you a hand?"

"Oh, yes… yes, thanks, that would be good. Not sure what has happened really. Just can't seem to get it to print."

"Let me just have a look for you."

She probably hasn't pressed the start button. New starters tend not to do the obvious.

"Anyway, my name is Maxwell. I am just down the end of the floor."

"Oh hi, Maxwell. My name is Jane. Just started this morning."

"How's it going so far then? You need a piece of string to find your way back to the front door in this building, don't you?"

She lets out a really loud laugh, a bit disproportionate to the quality of the joke. Again, new starter nerves kicking in.

"Who is your buddy?" I say.

A buddy is not like a buddy in the real world. It has a specific meaning in this office. It is essentially another office worker, usually in a more senior position, who is tasked with guiding the new starter. Like a go-to person. For precisely in a situation like this when you can't work out how to use the printer.

"Oh yes, so that is Jim. He is really nice. Made me feel very welcome."

"Oh yes, Jim. I know Jim," I say. So will she come to know Jim in time. "Anyway, let's see if we can't sort this issue out for you, I say."

It's a paper jam. Paper jams are a strange one. They seem to divide office workers into two groups. Some respond to a paper jam by immediately contacting the

IT department. But by the time you get back to your desk, log the complaint on the IT troubleshooting website, and wait for IT to deploy their team to resolve the issue, the original purpose of printing the item would more than likely be lost. And then there is the other category of have-a-go office workers, who have a go at unblocking the paper jam themselves. The printer even drops a few hints. It tells you which tray the paper jam is in with a flashing diagram on the dashboard.

It is generally quite normal for all new starters by default to fall into the first category, i.e. panic and contact IT. The fact that Jane hasn't seen the big flashing sign on the top of the printer saying 'paper jam' is probably just down to new starter panic.

"So the issue is a paper jam in tray two. So, if you take the drawer out, usually you can see a piece of paper causing the problem. Let's take a look," I say, trying hard not to come across a little patronising. Sure enough, there is a mangled piece of paper in the tray. I pull it out. No need for any IT technicians to be deployed.

"Oh great, thanks. That's much appreciated. Thanks again."

After waiting for a further couple of minutes for the new starter to find the dispatch tray, I log on to my print job. Ah, for fuck's sake. The printer is out of paper. Jane just had the last of it.

26

I Enjoy Walking My Dog

Back at my desk I now have 3.5 minutes to review eight CVs. On screen, as I couldn't print them. Skim-reading CVs means just reading the first and last sections of the CVs. Missing out the middle section. The middle section is usually all about examples or their work experiences and qualifications. I will have to give that a miss. The juicy bits are in the preamble and the 'other interests' section. The preamble section is the intro. The bit where the applicant makes a general statement about themselves and why they are suitable for the role. There is usually a lot a bollocks written in those sections.

I have a skim read of the CVs preambles. 'Committed, dedicated, effective communicator, willing to learn, prepared to go the extra mile...' And a personal favourite of mine 'exceptional interpersonal skills'. What does that mean? By whose standard is that to be judged? Smacks a little of arrogance to me. There is a fine line between confidence and arrogance.

One of the CVs does have a new one on me. 'Unique, commercially-driven and focused individual.'

I haven't seen that one before. I am interested for a second. Not for long though.

The 'other interests' section, though, is the section that tends to house the most interesting moments. This is the section where applicants can express themselves, list their hobbies, give a snapshot of their personality, their life outside the office. The section not to be boring. Even if you are boring in real life, you need to not be boring here. What do we have here then with this lot?.

'I enjoy walking.' I have seen that one many times before. I never get the point of it. I don't see how that would enhance any office. I think most people who put down that they enjoy walking have in their minds a more vigorous type of walking. You know, the kind of walking you do on a Sunday afternoon before hitting the pub for a Sunday carvery. Rambling is another word for it, I think. Nice sentiment, but advanced walking techniques probably don't actually help much in an office environment. The activities that involve walking within the confines of the office environment are limited. Ironically, putting down 'enjoys sitting for prolonged periods' probably makes more sense. That would get my attention. Strange, I don't think I have ever seen that one. If I did, in my world they would be fast-tracked to the top table.

Quite closely connected to 'enjoying walking' is 'enjoying eating'. *Who doesn't?* would be my thoughts on that. My advice to any prospective candidates who have bent my ear over the years as to the best activities to put on the 'other interests' section here is generally not to put in this section a hobby or activity that if you didn't carry it out regularly, you would die.

Next CV, and another classic: 'Enjoys spending time with friends and family.' Straight out of the CV top ten playbook. That one is, however, a negative in my book. If that is what they like to do, the applicant is way more likely to leave on the dot of 5pm to get home to do just that. I have less of a problem with that when you have twenty years' experience as an office worker behind you, than as a new starter.

2.31pm

I am running a bit late so I put in a bit of a shift down the stairs to the presentation room. I open the door. Eight fresh faces are staring at me. None of them say a word. Most of them are looking terrified. A couple of them are looking a bit smug. You always get a couple of smuggies. I have mentally discarded them already.

This room is way too big for eight people. I thought this would look stupid. Why has Felix booked this room? The presentation room is designed to hold a capacity of about fifty people. It looks like the Proclaimers trying to play Wembley stadium. It just makes them look pathetic.

I need to do a quick health and safety headcount. It isn't going to take long given that there are eight of them. The first test is to make sure they can spell their names on the register on the way in. I have a glance at them, looking all serious. I feel a bit like a teacher. Could probably do with some spectacles so I can really look down on them for the full headmaster effect. There seem to be eight people all signed in.

"Hello all," I start simply. "My name is Maxwell. This is just a short presentation on behalf of the firm, to give you an idea of what we do and so we can start to get to know you all. It won't take long. Just maybe twenty-five to thirty minutes, with the opportunity for questions at the end. Also, you may need to bear with me as I am filling in for a colleague who unfortunately was pulled away on an assignment at the last minute."

I carry on in total autopilot, not believing a word of what I am saying. But I owe it to these kids to be vaguely sincere. They are at the start of their corporate journey. Who am I to dampen their fires?

I think I have got better over the years at office presentations. I used to be bad. Nervy. I was so bad when I was starting that I used to occasionally imbibe some moonshine before giving presentations. Using alcohol to get you through a presentation is a delicate balance though. A bit of alcohol can work wonders. Get the quantity right, the nerves fall away, and no one knows you have had a drink. It is generally performance-enhancing. The shackles are off. But stray onto the wrong side of that hill, and it is a bumpy ride to the bottom.

So it didn't take me long to realise that alcohol couldn't be a long-term solution. In my wilderness years of trying to find the solution to my presentation nerves, I looked to other non-chemical-based inspirations. 'Just imagine your audience naked' was a common one. 'Scuse me?

The other popular one is to not make eye contact with anyone in the room but to stare at some point above all their heads on the back wall. Won't this make you come across as a little unhinged? Just staring madly at a spot on the back of the wall. Not even blinking. Just looking like a man possessed. That surely won't relax either you or your audience. No. Simply put, presentations, probably much like many things in life, become easier with age and experience.

I could really be saying anything though. I could be talking about the best albums from the 1980s and these guys would still be hanging on my every word. Their only concern is to look interested.

An hour later…
Still talking.

An hour and 20 minutes later…
Slightly overshot my presentation there, but nearly at the end now.

"So, I hope that gives you an idea of what we do. Any questions?"

Initially, I am met with a wall of silence. I have either covered every topic under the sun or, more likely, they haven't a fucking clue about anything that I have just said.

27

Lads Holiday?

It is about 8.45am and I am chatting to Noah over a cappuccino in the coffee house.

"So Maxwell, how's things? You got a spring in your step today?"

"Never until I see you, my friend, you know that… Yes, I think I do actually. I might try some oat milk today if you have any."

"I beg your pardon?"

"You heard. Oat milk. The one that doesn't come from a cow."

"I know what oat milk is, Maxwell. Just never heard you ask for it. You on a diet then?"

"Not really, but no harm in trying something different once in a while."

"How long is that going to last then?"

"At least until tomorrow, Noah."

"That's good, 'cause we don't have any oatmilk."

"You don't? You are cutting out a big market there, mate."

"Maxwell, just to remind you again – I don't own the place. I don't have shares in the company that owns it or anything similar. And do you know the result of all that?"

I shrug.

"It means, my friend, that I don't have any influence on what goes on the menu. My role is to open up, serve you and the seven other regulars, and then lock up."

"We should swap jobs for a day."

"You couldn't hack this job, Maxwell."

"Hey, I worked in a sweet shop when I was a kid. Wasn't too bad at it either."

"Anyway, let's get to the important stuff. How are you going on the ladies front? Any interest?"

"Not interested, Noah. That ship has sailed. You know that."

"That ship has sailed at your age? Piss off. You got loads of open road ahead. Get back in the game."

"You can talk. You haven't even been in the game. Your longest relationship is about two weeks as far as I know. Anyway, what's with you and that purple-haired lady from a few weeks back?"

"Eh?"

"You know. A couple of weeks ago. That suited and booted girl. Purple hair. You were fixated. So fixated that you didn't notice me go arse over tit on your doorstep. The one that stepped over me when I was lying on your doorstep."

"Oh, the purple-haired lady who stepped over you when you were lying on the doorstep on your back? I remember now," Noah says sarcastically. "I did notice actually. I came out to help you. So did the purple-haired lady."

"Oh that's right, after about five minutes of your gazing into her eyes. Could have died from a brain hemorrhage. Anyway, what's the story with the lady then, Noah?"

"No idea, really. Think she works in an office like you. That's what she said anyway."

"Yeah I got a bit of an office vibe from her. Looks a bit like managerial material."

"So Maxwell, we have been friends for a little while. Well, acquaintances at least. Would you agree?"

"Yes."

"So do you trust me to tell you the truth?"

"I suppose. You are scaring me now."

"Maxwell, you need to pick your game up a bit. You are approaching fifty?"

"Eh? I am forty-one!"

"As I said, not that far away from fifty. You have been working at the same place your whole life. Coming in here as long as I can remember. Nothing wrong with that, you know that. I like seeing you." Noah looks a bit serious. "But since the split... you know, with Mandy... you have been treading water. You can't fool me. You pretend like it is all OK. Are you though? Really? Life goes on, my friend. Like I said, maybe you need to just get out there a bit more."

I hate it when Maxwell gets all serious. I feel like he is about to talk at me for a bit and not to me...

"I am keeping it all going, Noah."

"You need to be doing more than keeping it together. If you carry on down this route then even your own shadow will get bored and piss off. Hey, I have an idea. Why don't me and you book a lads' holiday. South of France somewhere. Or maybe Magaluf."

Jesus, why does everyone want to go to Magaluf? "The problem, Noah, is that we aren't lads. So I'm not sure the stuff you should be doing on a lads' holiday would be very good at this stage of life."

"Answer me this, Maxwell. When is the last time you celebrated your birthday? I mean *really* celebrated your birthday."

"What's the point in celebrating your birthday after thirty-five, Noah? What did you do at your last birthday? Play pass the parcel and musical chairs? Don't hold back, Noah, will you?"

"I won't. That's what proper friends are for. You would tell me the same."

"OK, let's go to Ibiza in the summer. You can bring the day glow bands and beanie hat. Anyway, gotta get to the office. Can't be late."

Just as I leave, Noah shouts at me. "And just one more thing, Maxwell."

"Haven't you done enough emotional damage for one day?"

"Great shave today. You must be putting some pennies in your electricity meter."

I grin. But as I leave the coffee shop I think for a second. Noah has just ever so slightly ripped me apart emotionally. Is he right? Maybe he is right. Have birthdays now just become the anniversary of the day I was born? Do I need to put myself about some more? There are more questions than answers.

28

The Office Slurper

"So Maxwell, how are you feeling?," Lennox says at the start of another lunchtime session.

How did I know he was going to say that?

"Not bad, Lennox. Trying to do a bit more exercise. Eat a bit healthier. Sleep a bit more." That will impress him.

"Good, all of that is good for the body. And what's good for the mind is good for the body."

"And what is good for the body is good for the mind," I say.

"You have got it, Maxwell. You wouldn't believe what a difference lifestyle has on mood. Has your sleep got any better then? Have you cut out the grapes in the middle of the night?" Lennox laughs.

"Yeah, I know that probably came across a bit weird."

"Not really, Maxwell. There isn't much I haven't been told between these four walls. Anyway today I want to talk about stuff that irritates you. You will understand why later. I do this with a lot of my clients. Mild anxiety tends to induce getting easily irritated."

"What, like when you have cut your hair and all the bits get in your collar?" I say.

Lennox laughs. "No. Although that is annoying obviously. There is not much any therapist can do about hair down your back. No, I was thinking about people induced irritations. People that annoy you. Things that annoy you. Things that you have to do that annoy you. Things that you aren't able to do that annoy you. Anything really. As long as it annoys you."

"The office slurper," I say, without having to think.

"The office slurper?"

"Yes, the office slurper."

"Tell me about the office slurper."

"So, this guy at work, every time he has a drink – and he has a lot of drinks– he slurps. I am not talking about normal slurping. This is extreme, unnecessary, violent slurping. There is no respite from it. No time in between slurps to give you time to recover. He takes several slurps in a row. I mean multiple slurps. Perhaps seven or eight in a row."

"OK, so why does this annoy you so much?"

I think for a moment.

"I think it is a mixture of two things. The first being that it is… well, quite honestly it is a bit selfish really. *He* might be oblivious to it, but all of us around him certainly aren't. But more than that. I just can't understand the need for it, Lennox, if truth be told."

"What do you mean, Maxwell, when you say you can't understand the need for it? Describe your feelings here."

"What I mean is, what is the science behind slurping? What's the medical case for it? Making a drink so hot that his lips can't take it, so he has to create a suction effect with his mouth so that the liquid contact with the inside of his lips is minimised. And if the liquid is so hot that you need to make sure that it doesn't contact the inside of your lips, what in God's name is it doing to your insides?"

"So, you can't control that individual and what he is doing, and what noises he may or may not be generating. But what you can control is your *reaction* to it. That is what this is about."

"Yeah, probably true Lennox. But you should try sitting there when he is on one."

"Ok but there is another way of looking at this, Maxwell. As we know, there is more than one way of looking at anything in life. Often the way we look at something is the problem, not the thing in the first place. For example, have you considered that it may be a medical condition bringing about the slurping, far-fetched as that might be? Would that change the way you viewed the slurping?"

Only Lennox can find a way to justify really bad slurping. But that's why I am sitting on his sofa. That's the place I would quite like to get to. I am probably still a long way off, but hopefully at least I have boarded the train to tranquility city.

"Yeah, I get that I suppose," I say.

"It's like when we talked general anxiety. Anxiety, irritation, anger issues, whatever they might be. They all stem from the same place. Chasing a thought, an emotion."

"Yeah OK, I see that a bit. So how do I avoid that thinking then."

"That is what takes time. And we are working on it. But just as a start, so next time you are in that situation, try to focus on other matters. Basically, don't analyse the science behind why people may or may not slurp. What you aren't going to do is actually stop people slurping in the first place. Control the stuff within your control, Maxwell. Maybe consciously shift your focus to something else going on in the office at that point."

I decide to give that tactic a try.

3.40pm the same day...

"And in all seriousness, are you saying that shit to me with a straight face? You should be ashamed of yourself. You haven't a fucking clue how a business should treat its customers. Distasteful, really distasteful." Back in the office and Trevor is on a consumer complaint rant again.

I am trying to deploy what Lennox told me to do at lunch. Distraction techniques. I think I need Lennox to sit next to me at work. A bit like a personal trainer.

Somewhere over to my left I can hear Felix, the office greasy pole climber. He must be at some unfortunate office worker's desk again, subjecting them to his version of white noise. Sounds like he is talking to a customer on the phone.

"Hey Richie, its Felix," Felix says. Slight pause.

"Felix," says Felix.

Another pause.

"Felix Doberman from the office."

Another pause.

"I came out to see you last week," Felix says. Another pause.

"I had a red anorak on and a blue tie," Felix says.

I can barely contain my laughter. This chap clearly hasn't a clue who Felix is. Felix must be seething.

I look at Daniel. We both grin. "Hilarious," Daniel says.

For once I agree with him.

29

Health and Safety

One of the health and safety crew is on the office floor. You can spot them a mile away. They rarely smile and carry a clipboard around, capturing even the most minor breach of health and safety legislation. Some of this I can understand – checking the smoke alarms, checking there is foam in the fire extinguishers, and so on. But they are also on the hunt for slouching. Office workers slouching at their desks, to be more precise. I don't think this interest in our back health is out of the goodness of their little hearts. I think some office worker a few years ago successfully sued their employer for a really bad back allegedly caused by not being told not to slouch at work consistently.

I am a bit of a serial sloucher. I have been slouching for years. Each year I am getting a millimetre or two closer to my keyboard. One day my face will be operating the keyboard. But health and safety are on the prowl. Time to sit up a little straighter then. No swinging back on my chair either.

I feel them pass somewhere behind me. I can't hear any scribbling, so I may have got through this assessment. I'll hear about it soon enough if I haven't.

4.50pm

Just about to log off for another day. I suddenly get a text from Wendy. It says can I call her as soon as possible. That isn't like Wendy. I call straight away.

"Maxxie."

"Yes, eh up Wendy. You OK? Got yer text."

"Yeah, not too bad. Just need to let you know that, I need to go down south to see my folks tomorrow. My dad isn't doing too well at the moment. Under doctor's orders to stay at home, and my mum needs a bit of help looking after him at the moment. So just to say you have got the run of the house for a few weeks."

"Oh OK, Wendy. Hope yer Dad is OK. Don't worry about me."

"But that's just it, Max, I do worry about you."

"Hey come on, I can put my own music on as loud as I want and leave my plates in the sink, and I won't be disturbed by you coming in from work every day when I am just about to get up. Reckon I will be OK."

"Yeah, whatever Maxxie. Just make sure you have a shower at least once every two days, you filthy git."

"OK Wendy. See you when you get back. Keep me posted. Love to your folks."

5.30pm

I'm on the train home. I am listening to the radio on my AirPods. Occasionally I listen to the radio. I like the smooth chill channel. But today I want to keep abreast of world events. So that is BBC Radio 4. It used to be BBC Radio 1 until I hit about twenty-nine, at which point it was pointed out to me by someone that no-one entering their fourth decade listened to Radio 1. I tried BBC Radio 2 for a while, but that just seemed like a dumbed down version of Radio 1. BBC Radio 3? I have never met any other person who either listens to that channel or knows what it plays. It is like the best quiz question ever.

"So what does BBC Radio 3 feature?" There would be complete silence. Even from advanced quiz aficionados.

The last item on the 5.30 news catches my attention though.

Newsreader: *And finally, we have reports of efforts by the Chinese authorities to contain an outbreak of an as yet unidentified virus in the province of Wuhan. It is reported that several people have been affected by the virus, which has in some instances caused fatalities. It is unclear where the virus emanated from, but reports suggest it is highly infectious and has started to spread through the surrounding community. China is, we understand, putting stern containment measures in place that it hopes will isolate the virus from wider growth.*

Shit. That doesn't sound good.

30

Mr Washbeard

My desk phone is ringing. My desk phone hardly ever rings. Most people use the work mobiles now. There is a certain class of person that uses the landline. Generally they are over 55 years of age. I know the number immediately. Just when I was mentally winding down for today. One of my more challenging customers. This is another issue with the open-plan office. You can't just ignore calls. Now every office-working Tom, Dick and Sally knows if you are dropping a call. Even with my phone on the lowest setting.

I let it ring three times.

It isn't ringing off. I am forced to answer.

"Hello, Mr Washbeard." I finally pick the phone up on seven rings. "How are you? Well, I hope." I immediately know why he is calling. It is always a complaint. Mr Washbeard has too much time on his hands. Way too much time. And lots of money. Any man with that much time on his hands and a lot of money is dangerous. Time means that people can analyse, scrutinise, pre-meditate and plot. Not dissimilar to a despot.

So in summary, Mr Washbeard is a dangerous man, even if he is at the end of a phone, and is an even more significant threat to a rushed-off-his-feet forty-something office worker.

"Well, I thought I was, Mr Orwellian, until I got your belated invoice through this morning. Not happy about that, to be honest with you. Not at all happy about that. I thought I was fully paid up on the current contract, and then I go and get this bill out of the blue. Two main problems with that, Mr Orwellian."

Just two problems, I think. That isn't actually too bad for Mr Washbeard.

"Oh OK, sorry. So what are those?" I say, putting on the required professional office voice.

"First, the invoice has my old address. How many times have I called in to give you my updated address? Why aren't you updating the system? Surely there is a whole load of data-protection issues thrown up from that."

"Yes, I can only apologise on behalf of the company, Mr Washbeard. I will make sure credit control amends your address on their system."

Blaming it on credit control is always my get-out-of-jail-free card. Ninety percent of customer complaints are to do with billing and invoices. And most of the billing is generated by credit control. Actually, control is probably not the most appropriate word for their department. Most of the time 'out of control' would probably be more like it. I feel a bit sorry for them. Actually, I think I would sooner be a member of HR or the accounts department than credit control. Poor sods. Just either being shouted at or shouting at other people all day long...

"…and the second problem is that there are all these added costs on the bill that I haven't agreed before signing the contract. I need a proper breakdown of the costs here. Not just dates and numbers."

I have pretty much switched off at this point. Fifteen years in the office has I think – or at least, I hope – given me the grace and experience to withstand this kind of barrage. I must have learned something over the years. As a young office worker, I would have already kicked off by now. I would already have threatened to rip his face off by about this precise moment in the exchange, whilst booting my office chair across the room with my really polished office shoes. But one of the few benefits of a loss of office worker innocence is that you learn strategies to control these situations. Occasionally maybe even turning an aggressive client to your way of thinking. To be able to control an angry, out-of-control person in the space of a meeting or phone call is the holy grail that all office workers aspire to. Like making a mad security dog lick your face. That's what you want. You want the dog to lick your face. And over the years, I've started to exercise techniques designed to subdue this kind of rage.

Noah told me a story once that has helped me in these type of specific work related verbal volleys.

Noah got stuck in a bar in the outback of Australia when he was on a gap year with his mates. Some locals, fueled by drink and drugs, started having a go. Noah was on his own, minding his own business, having a quiet drink and listening to some thrash metal music – which is, as I understand it, his preferred musical genre. But these morons kept pushing. Kept trying to push his buttons. Wouldn't leave it alone. Noah didn't react though. Didn't rise to it. Even when one of them pushed him, he still didn't rise to it. Some of this was self-preservation. There were quite a few of them and just one Noah. But still he didn't rise to it. In the end they got bored. There was no escalation. Noah's take on it was this: if someone has a go at you, then don't react, just be nice. If someone continues to have a go at you, just continue to be nice. Don't react. And so on and so forth. Until eventually it is time not to be nice. You will generally know when the point arrives. That's what Noah reckons anyway. Not that I could picture that man ever knowing when it might be time to not be nice. But there is a line. As long as that line is quite a long way set back though, all should be good and right with the world.

I don't think I need to employ that technique here though with Mr Washbeard. The second technique might be more relevant here. That would be to find my mental happy place. Mr Washbeard continues on his tirade. Visualisation. Lennox gave me this technique I think at one of our sessions; part of the mindfulness and meditation techniques, I believe. I am trying to go there now. In my brain at least. To my happy place. I am in the South of France, on a lilo somewhere off the coast. I am in crystal clear blue waters. The sun is hot but not too hot. The kind of heat that you enjoy without burning, even if you are out in it for eight hours with no breaks. The lilo is the deluxe model, so that mainly means it comes equipped with a lager-decanting straw system, so I can drink wine whilst reclining. There is no one around me. I can hear just the very gentle swish of the ocean; shallow waves propelling towards shore, just making sure I don't drift out to sea and drown. Perfect. One of two sharks pass under my lilo but they are very tame, almost dolphin- like. There is no risk of shark bite at all from these fellas. And there, as I am still in visualisation mode, floating somewhere in the Mediterranean, I think I can still just about make out the drone of a late middle- aged man moaning on about some problem with a VAT invoice. It sounds like he is still on point two…

31

The Office Cycler Rises

An e-mail pops up from Tony, the office cyclist.

Maxwell, I am a little indisposed at the moment. Any chance you could just collect my document from the printer? I could do with it quite urgently. I have just printed it off.

Eh? This is odd.

What the hell are you on about? I e-mail in return, with an irritated e-mail emoji at the end. *I am happy to get your printing as long as while I am at it, you pop to the shop and get me some Maltesers and a packet of peanuts.*

I can't explain it now. Just get it for me, will you? he carries on. *I will explain later.*

Have you got cramp or something? I e-mail back.

At this point I see Tony's head popping up from behind his desk on the other side of the floor. His arms are gesticulating now in the direction of the printer. He seems to be getting a little frenzied. It does suddenly cross my mind that Tony might be in some genuine distress. Maybe some form of belated dehydration from not drinking enough on the cycle to work this morning. Maybe he needs some form of medical treatment. Maybe I am the last person to have e-mail communications with him as he succumbs to stroke or heart attack.

A few moments pass. Nothing further. No more messages.

And then I hear some slight rumblings of laughter in the distance. A few titters. I look up. Tony is making his way to the printer. The reason now becomes clear. He has forgotten his work trousers. What this means is that he still has on his bright yellow lycra. But he had tried to hide that all day with a suit and tie upper combo. I didn't know Tony would be so self-conscious. He isn't in the mornings. But he must have been sitting in his chair all morning like that. Poor sod. I could have got his printing for him. I feel bad now.

4.45pm that same day…
What is Daniel doing now? He is turning his laptop upside-down and shaking it. All kinds of shit is falling out of it. Probably old bits of food, dead skin and the like. All over his desk. This is his misguided idea of a tidy-up.

4.55pm
My contractual hours are nearly over for another working day. I press the shutdown button on my PC. A message pops up: 'Working on updates. Please do not shut down your system. One percent of 100% completed.' Bloody updates. Software updates. Always just exactly when you don't want them.

5.15pm
Twenty-four of 100% complete…

5.19pm

Thirty-six of 100% complete...

5.21pm

Forty-eight of 100% complete...

5.22pm

Forty-seven of 100% complete... (It is now going backwards – how is that even possible?)

The cleaner is on the floor with his Hoover. Nice chap. Always has his headphones on though whilst vacuuming under desks. They recently used a mobile hoover device. A kind of artificial intelligence hoover that worked I think on some form of sensors. I think someone nicked the one deployed on the 2nd floor though, so human cleaners were re-instated.

5.47pm

Updates complete.

But now the system wants to restart. Why restart the PC after updates? Let me restart in the morning. I want to go home. Another three minutes to wait so it can load up just so I can shut the thing down again. Here we go. Desktop loading, apps winding up. I have my finger on the cursor as soon as I see the power button. So what is with the updates then? Oh, there you go. A little weather gauge is added to the taskbar. Lovely. A cute little picture of a cloud with a temperature next to it. One degree Celsius and a chance of snow. Useful stuff.

32

Worrying in the Wrong Place

Lennox is in quite serious mode today, I can tell.

"So Maxwell, I want to move away a little bit from the CBT and mindfulness from the last few sessions and just explore in a little more depth issues around anxiety generally. Trying to understand a little more about anxiety, and how the mind works in relation to that."

"OK."

"So I have developed this little technique with my clients, which I think over the years has helped my clients to put stuff into perspective – to contextualise a situation, I like to call it."

"OK," I say.

"OK, so I want you to think back over your life and list your five greatest worries."

"Right. You mean any kind of worry?"

"Not worry when something has actually happened. I call that legitimate response worry. I mean worry about an event or thing that might or might not happen in the future. And it must be something that worried you for a while. Totally subjective to you. Doesn't matter if no one else in the world would worry about it, as long as it bothered you. That's the point. Something you couldn't shake off. Going down that little rabbit hole of worry."

"OK. Might just take a few moments to think of these, Lennox."

"Take your time, Maxwell."

"So probably first... that would be, I think, crashing my car into a bus. A bus full of passengers. Not deliberately obviously. An accident."

Lennox takes notes on his pad as he listens to me.

I pause for a bit, contemplating. How do you capture your top worries over the years. Not as easy as I would think, this. I have had my fair share of worries. Who hasn't? What is Lennox driving at here? Don't analyse Maxwell. Just do as the man says.

"Second... So I played this table tennis match a few years ago that I was expected to win. You know, ping-pong."

"Yes, I know what table tennis is, Maxwell."

"And I remember, to be honest... well, if you excuse my bad language, kind of shitting myself before playing the match. I don't know why. I had played loads of ping-pong before then."

Lennox is still scribbling.

"Next... and this one is a bit weird. But I went through a phase of worrying about what happened to the dinosaurs..."

I look to see if there is a reaction from Lennox to that one. Surely he is now thinking I am taking the piss.

Surely he hasn't heard that one before. Still nothing though. He just keeps writing notes.

"When I say worrying about what happened to the dinosaurs, I don't mean worrying about *them* as such, you know, in the sense that I might bump into one on my way to the office. No, what I mean is that from what I have read, it was some asteroid that hit the Earth that wiped them out. So as soon as I knew that, I think I went through a bout of worrying that the same thing might happen again."

I pause for a bit.

"But... so probably my biggest worry..."

"Go on."

I pause. This is starting to get serious.

"So I worry that this world – it isn't good enough for my daughter..."

This time Lennox does look up, gives a slight smile. "OK, Maxwell. So now, if you don't mind, I just want to look a bit deeper into those. OK, lets look at the table tennis match worry. What happened in the match that you should have won?"

"I lost."

"OK. So from what seem to be telling me, you were the better player, you were expected to win, but you lost. Can you remember why you lost?"

"Yes, I think I do. I was too nervous. Couldn't play properly."

"So nerves affected how you actually played?"

"Yes."

"And why did you feel so nervous?"

"I just couldn't handle the thought of losing. The

guy I was playing, he was a bit of dick. And his dad was a bit of a dick. I needed to win."

"So you needed to win so badly, and for reasons not really connected to the match itself. You made it too important in your mind, too personal?"

"Yes. Trying too hard. That was always the problem with me and ping-pong. Always better when you have nothing to lose. You are all loose and relaxed."

"Yeah, it's funny isn't it, Maxwell? Sometimes you can want things a little too much."

"Yes, all of that, I think."

"So what did you do?"

"I tanked it," I say.

"Tanked it? What is that?"

"Tanking in sport is basically when you give up. So that in the end you haven't actually lost," I say.

"'Cos you never tried in the first place."

"You got it, Lennox."

"And how did that make you feel afterwards?"

"Pretty shit. But actually, if I had tried and lost that would have been even worse."

"You know what, Maxwell? Someone once said to me that successful people hate to fail, but they aren't afraid to fail. Sounds like you were afraid to fail."

"Completely. I was shitting myself, like I said. Failing wasn't an option. But you know what? You can't fail if you don't try in the first place. Not that I am proud of any of that Lennox. That goes without saying."

"I think that must have come from some kind of insecurity when you were younger, which maybe turned into a bit of a lack of confidence. It came out when you played ping-pong".

"Yeah maybe. But it might have been self-inflicted also. What is it they say? Your greatest opponent in life is yourself. Something along those lines."

"Do you recall anything when you were younger that stayed with you?"

More thinking time.

"Erm… Yes so I used to like drama at school. You know, a bit of acting. Bit of role play. That kind of thing. And the pinnacle of that was the school play every year. All the mums and dads turned up. It was a bit of an occasion. And getting picked for the major parts in school plays was a big deal. All the kids wanted the big parts. I think I did anyway."

"OK, so what happened?"

"So for the school play that year – I think I must have been twelve or thirteen – the drama teacher told me I had made the cut. A big part. An important role. The centre of attention."

"OK, so that was positive, right Maxwell?"

"Well, you would think so, wouldn't you? But turns out this big pivotal, life-changing role that my drama teacher was banging on about was in fact playing a dead person for the whole of the play. Not talking, not singing, not dancing. Just lying there. Being dead. Acting being dead. I wouldn't have minded it so much if I was killed on stage. You know, like I had a large speaking part and then I had to act getting shot and dying. That would have been OK. But no. I was dead when I was brought on stage in the first place."

143

"Oh I see. OK, yes, there must have been some disappointment there. But maybe there is another way to look at this…" Lennox says.

"Jesus, Lennox, no. I have to stop you there. If there is one circumstance that you can't turn into a positive it is that. Playing a dead person in your childhood end of year play."

"OK, what about the other worries then? Lets take the bus one and the dinosaur/asteroid one. Those worries are to do with things that you think might happen. They are called anticipatory worries."

"Yes, OK," I say.

"And have either of them actually happened? Have you ever crashed into a bus before? Has an asteroid hit the Earth?"

"Err… no to all of those, I suppose."

"Maybe that is stating the obvious. And I know you probably know that. That's the thing with worry. Most people know that it doesn't do much good, but sometimes you can't stop it."

"Yeah," I say.

"So tell me something now that has actually happened that has been a problem. That genuinely bothered you at the time."

"Err. OK, so…" I think for a bit. "So probably the banking crisis of 2007."

"OK, and what was the significance of that for you?"

"Same as for everyone really. Fear of losing my job, mainly. The economy was in a shit state."

"Yes, I remember, Maxwell. Everyone was a bit worried I think. That was all very normal. But tell me, did you at any point prior to that crisis, at any point, worry that a banking crisis was just around the corner?"

"No, I can't say that I did."

"And that's my point, Maxwell. If you give it some more thought, I bet you could find a hundred things in your life that have happened, that might not have been very pleasant, but that you had never worried about before they happened. And on the flip side what follows is you have probably worried about even more things that, in actual fact have never actually happened, or if they have they have never been anywhere near as bad as you first thought."

"Yes, true. I see where you are coming from there."

"So I like to call this "worrying in the wrong place". It's a pretty obvious concept when you think about it. Thing is, very few of us do. I really like this technique. You can't really argue against the fact that worrying in the wrong place goes on all the time. Most of the time. Much more than worrying in the right place. Once your brain gets that, well, I think stuff gets a lot easier."

Sometimes, truth be told, I don't always get what Lennox is saying. Or I do get it, but don't really agree with it. But this one I like. Worrying in the wrong place? This session has ended on a positive. I may get a pint of lager shandy in the pub if I have time on my way back to the office.

Part 2

33

The Birth of the Locked-down Office Worker

Week 1

There has been a bit of an eerie silence for the last hour or so in the office. There is something afoot. Clare is pretending to work, but I think she has been marking up the in-flight menu from her last trip to Magaluf. Clive has just returned from the toilet. Daniel has been quiet for about the last 20 minutes or so. Takes a lot to keep that boy silent.

"I don't like the look of this chaps" Daniel says.

"Whats that Daniel?" says Clive.

"Just looking at the stock market. It's plunging. Something big is brewing, the stock market doesn't lie."

The stock market doesn't lie? Where has Daniel got that from?

"You mean this virus?" Clive says.

"Yeah. This shit coming out of China. Some moron has eaten a bat." Daniel says.

"What without cooking it?" I say.

"I don't think it makes a difference as to whether

the bat was cooked, marinated, or nuked Maxwell" says Clive.

"So what plans for the weekend all?" I say trying to lighten the mood slightly.

"Going to my sisters" says Clare. "Haven't seen her in ages. She has just had a new baby."

"Ah that's great Clare. Pass on my congratulations. Boy or girl?"

"Girl. She already has three though."

Fucking hell four children? I didn't cope having one.

Suddenly there is a global office e-mail from Management. This is addressed to the whole firm. Not just a department or office – this is to the whole firm. Usually this is to do with the launch of some new firm-wide software product, or sending us a £25 gift voucher as a Christmas bonus.

But this one has 'URGENT' written in the header. As far as I can recall, I have never seen a global management e-mail addressed like that. Not ever.

The e-mail reads:

Dear all,

You will of course have heard much on the news recently relating to the spread of the new Covid-19 virus. We have been monitoring the position very carefully. The position now is that we understand that the government will very shortly be issuing a statement requesting people to enter a period of what is to effectively be, a form of lockdown.

This may mean that attendance at the office will be prohibited. We understand that this might be necessary to control the spread of this new virus.

Until then we await further government guidelines. However, as a responsible employer, we have decided to, and with immediate effect, request that all staff do not attend the office for the foreseeable future. We are also shutting the office as of now and asking you all to go home immediately.

There is a time to swear. And there are many more times not to swear. This is a time to swear. I read the e-mail again. And again. And then again. I am looking at the words but they just aren't sinking in. This isn't real. This feels like something out of a horror film. Office workers being ordered to leave the office? We have been sent home before. Usually at about 4.45pm on Christmas Eve, fifteen minutes or so before the end of our contractual hours as a Christmas gift from Management. And once when the "Beast from the East" snowstorm struck. But not for a virus. And not for the "*foreseeable*".

We are all looking at each in bewilderment. Clive is not biologically programmed to get flustered, but I can tell in his eyes his feathers are well and truly flustered. Clare is immediately thinking about getting a last minute flight out to Magaluf. And Daniel has remained quiet.

Being ordered to stop working because of a virus? Not anything close to approaching that in my working lifetime. This says 'for the foreseeable future'. These words have never come from Management before, not as long as I can remember. Not in any context, let alone in the context of people not working. For a company that only exists in the end to make net profits, these words mean complete and total, unadulterated panic.

We are being instructed to go home by the Conservative Party, and it seems, to stay at home. *To Stay at Home.*

I read the e-mail once again. I am starting to hear the chatter around the office. It is starting to move from a dull hum to a crescendo of noise. People are moving around, talking to other office workers.

Clive is the first to start to regain some of his usual composure. "I am sure this won't be for long. Just some short term containment programme. A bit like when Sars hit a few years ago. I seem to remember there was quite a lot of brewhaha about that too. Blew over really quite quickly though if I recall."

Fuck that, I am taking myself off home. Straight home. I am not going to pass go and I am definitely not going to collect £100.

"Ok chaps so I am gonna do as instructed and remove myself for the foreseeable" I say.

"Me too Max" Daniel says. "I don't like the look of this. See you all on the other side, hopefully."

6pm later that day
There were loads of ashen faces on the train on my way home. This was not the usual commuter train home. There wasn't much chatting going on. Just a lot of staring out the window. Reminded me very much of the train home in South London just after the planes had hit the twin towers in New York on 11 September

2001. There are certain events in life that transcend anything. Pivotal moments. Game-changing moments. This feels like another one of those.

I flip on the TV. The Prime Minister is holding an emergency news conference.

Wendy has a drinks cabinet in the house. I tend not to use it, apart from maybe on a Friday or Saturday night. Currently, though, the door to the drinks cabinet is half-open. Just in case I need it in a bit.

On the TV there is the Union Jack and then three podiums out front.

Boris Johnson, our current leader, makes his way to the front of the first podium. Two others come out and go left and right. Boris's podium is more forward than the other though obviously. This set up looks a little like the worst Olympic Games ceremony presentation ever, and with the worst athletes that country could possibly produce. Boris has been in the hot seat for a few months. The last time I saw him on TV before becoming the big cheese, he was presenting *Have I Got News for You* and getting the piss taken out of him. He is now at the podium. He could have at least brushed his hair and straightened his tie. Messy git. The supreme office worker. Our current leader. The standard all office workers should be striving to. With the hair of a wino after a night out.

"Hello," he starts.

"We will beat this thing," is how he ends.

What is in between is just mind-blowing. A dangerous, highly transmittable virus spreading like wildfire. A potential pandemic. A world problem. And the upshot? Jesus Christ, the upshot of all this… The upshot is that we are all to be put into an enforced lockdown. A lockdown? A fucking lockdown? This is the kind of stuff you see in the movies. Stay at home. Shut your windows. Find an old World War II bunker somewhere under your back garden. Get into your panic rooms and lock the doors.

We are being told to stay at home all day, every day. Not just the office. That's the least of anyone's concerns suddenly. No trips to bingo. No clubbing. No socialising. No therapy sessions with Lennox. You can only go out of your house for absolutely essential stuff. Basically rice and beans. And it doesn't stop there. When you are out getting your essential foods, you have to keep your distance from people. Don't mix bodily fluids in any circumstances. Just some of the craziest instructions you can ever possibly imagine. Offices shut until further notice. Not for a day or a week. Offices shut. Indefinitely. Office workers to work from home.

I am not in the best of states with this announcement. This is not a time to have any form of anxiety, whether that be mild, moderate or severe. The first thing I think about: my daughter, Evie. I don't even know where she is. I am in panic mode now. I text her. Make sure she is OK.

What am I supposed to do next? The drinks cabinet door is now fully open. In fact, I rip the door off its hinges. I pour a triple brandy. Might be more; I am not a barman. What I am though, is in complete and total fucking panic mode. I could do with Wendy right now. She would know the right thing to say. I put a towel over my head and fall asleep on my sofa sitting upright.

34

The Day After the Night Before (Second day of Lockdown)

I am still asleep. Still dreaming I think. I should be at work. I am in a dark room somewhere. Really dark. I can't see anything. There is just a slightly hazy light on the other side of the room. I can't quite make it out. There is some smoke coming from it. What is it? Light with some smoke coming out of it? It is getting bigger and bigger like it is coming towards me. Bloody hell. I can't move. I am shackled. I am at this thing's mercy. It gets bigger and bigger. I still can't make it out. Oh my God, what is it? The light is bright now. It seems to be... yes, yes, I think it is... it is a train. The front of a train. It has 8.08 on the front. This is my usual train to work. It is heading right at me. My own commuter train heading right for me. Turning on it's own kind. Jesus, someone wake me up.

The train is getting closer. I still can't move. This is it. The end is in sight. It is true what they say then – that you do see a bright light at the end, just before the ascension.

There is a bright light. But this isn't a light to the gates of eternal life. I can't see any angels here. In fact… no, it can't be. This is too much. This can't be how I meet my maker. It is… yes it is… Jim from Accounts' face is on the front of the train, grinning and laughing like a deranged banshee, revelling in my impending doom. I can't move. I can't run. Why can't you ever fucking run in a nightmare?

The train is about to hit. Jim's face is all I can see now in my entire field of vision. No, please… noooooo…

9.34am

I wake up. My bedclothes are soaked. I am still on the sofa. The TV is still on. My mind starts to panic.

9.34am? I should have been at my desk for thirty-four minutes already. What's happened to my usual biological clock? What's happened to my usual office morning routine? Hold on… something is not right. I pause. I think. I shake my head left and right. And then it hits me. Hits me like the train with Jim from Accounts' face on it. *We aren't going into the office. Not now. Not for the foreseeable.*

This is a movie still, surely. I am not properly awake. Still in some form of dreamworld. Someone pour lukewarm water over my face and wake me up, please. This can't be reality. This is the kind of awful B-movie that you can only see on the remotest and weirdest of cinema apps. But this may be real. I wipe my eyes. My phone will tell the story. I switch it on.

The social media headlines confirm it. What happened last night is real. Stay indoors. Escape the virus. OK. I need to get a grip. What do I need to check first? That's right. Fuck social media. Fuck the news. I need to check Evie is OK. Shit, please say she has texted back. Ah, thank the Lord. Yes she has. A quick text saying she is OK. She is somewhere in the south of France. She is travelling with a friend and they are both OK, in a rented place somewhere. I think of her mother also. Briefly and just for a moment.

I wander downstairs, still in a daze. The hangover isn't helping. This is a Tuesday. I don't drink on a school night. Not ever. But I did last night. I think I might carry on this afternoon. All the rules have suddenly gone out the window.

I am still in my dressing gown. On any other ordinary day, I would be in the office by now. I should be at least forty minutes or so into my day. Admittedly, I probably wouldn't have done anything productive at this point, but that isn't the point. I would still be actually in the office. I should be at the office. Sitting at my desk. Possibly with raised blood pressure readings from having to listen to Daniel's office banter. But at home in my dressing gown isn't where I am meant to be at this time on a Tuesday. Today is clearly no ordinary day.

I have my work phone with me. I'll see if there have been any work e-mails. No. None. Nothing. Just complete e-mail radio silence.

A text pops up. It's from Wendy. The text reads:

Maxxie. Awful, all this stuff going on. Stay well and safe. My dad is doing a bit better so hoping to be back home in a week or so. I need to be back to

the hospital in a week or so anyway with all this
Covid stuff kicking off. Look after yourself xx

I text back: *Love you, Wendy*

I grab four beers from the fridge, go back to bed and pull the covers over me.

35

Third Day of Lockdown

9.35am

I wake up in my dressing gown. There seems to be part of a half-eaten microwave only kebab on my stomach. The other half is on the floor. The kebab that is. I look to my left at my wardrobe. My office uniform is still hanging up. But there are no shirts, nicely ironed and pressed. No fresh pants and socks laid out on the floor.

9.55am

There is a new worry doing the rounds. Not just the virus. There is some chatter on the media outlets about shops possibly running out of food. Something to do with trauma in the supply chains and people panic-buying essential items. This is getting even more farcical. Surely we aren't at war? Or are we? Is this some elaborate government ruse to mask an alien invasion? That sounds far-fetched. But then so is a fucking worldwide pandemic. What was it that Lennox said about worry? What was the phrase? That's it – 'worrying in the wrong place'. If ever that applied.

I don't think anyone considered sane and measured would have been worrying about a worldwide pandemic.

That would have previously been the chatter of crack- heads and conspiracy theorists. Maybe me and Noah over a morning medium latte. But I think this might be real. Is this the human equivalent of the asteroid for the dinosaurs? My anxiety has now smashed through the roof.

I hope Noah is OK. What will he be making of this? The days of the leisurely morning coffee with complementary banter seem like they're from a different time. Truly you do not know what you have until it is gone. I haven't got Noah's number though. We spoke in real life. Only at the coffee house. We didn't text. That wasn't the nature of our relationship.

And what about Lennox? I think I have paid in advance for about another fifteen sessions. If there is ever a time for Lennox, it is now.

I call Lennox. The phone is ringing. It goes straight to voicemail though. "Hello, this is Lennox. We are very sorry, but at the moment, with the Covid-19 pandemic, we are not available for consultations or new appointments at this time. Sorry for any inconvenience caused. Please stay safe."

Shit. I don't even have Lennox at the moment. This is a lonely place to be.

1pm

Listening to the news. It is all about food shortages now. In full on panic mode I grab my car keys, and floor the car to the local Co-op.

There is hardly anyone in the shop. That isn't necessarily uncommon. I need some essentials. I suppose

160

everyone's interpretation of 'essentials' is different. For me, the 'essentials' are currently, and not necessarily in this order, milk, bread, eggs, and reduced-price white wine.

There aren't many people in the shop when I get there. The ones who are, are behaving oddly. As I pass, a couple of them look at me. It is a look I don't think I have ever seen before in my time on this planet, certainly from different people at the same time and in a shop. It is somewhere between confusion, mistrust and fear. Like I have two heads or something. Like I might just be about to kill their cat. I make a beeline for the bread and milk aisles, take as much bread and milk as I can carry, do a quick detour to the alcohol section and then speed to the till, trying to hold my breath for much of the way.

The lady serving me has a mask on. A fucking *mask*. I have only ever seen these worn in China and on *Casualty*. Now my local grocer is wearing a mask.

"Is that all, love?" she says as I drop my essentials down on the till.

"Oh, sorry, you can't take more than three milks," she says.

"Seriously?" I ask.

"Yes, sorry love, new shop rules. Rationing to stop panic bulk-buying."

Christ, there is a queue bubbling up behind me.

"And also, just to let you know," the assistant carries on, I think, although I can't quite hear her behind the mask she is wearing. I lean in to try to hear her. She moves back.

161

"So we aren't taking cash either. Just cards. That will be ten pounds fifty."

"Stay safe," she says as I grab my shopping and take flight. *Stay safe?* I think. It's one thing Wendy saying that, but the local Co-op shop assistant? I am not sure how to take this. It sounds more like something a captain in the army would say before sending a young recruit into a war zone. Certainly not something that you want to hear in your local store.

3.30pm

The afternoon since returning from the store has been a blur. I might have slept a bit, possibly drank a bit, and then immediately felt guilty about doing both. Sleep, drink and then guilt. I am back to my student days. Not in the way I would have liked though.

I still haven't done any work since we got sent home. I start to wonder how all my colleagues are doing. I start to think about them. Charlie, Tony, Jim, Daniel, Clive, Clare. Even Felix the office greasy pole climber. It occurs to me that, for all the time I have spent around them, I don't really know that much about any of their home lives.

Jim is married, I think. To another accountant maybe, which would be natural way of things. Dan is obviously single. Tony the office cyclist? I think he has a couple of grown-up daughters. Shit, what about Tim and Howard? How will they be able to work from home? Poor sods. Clive will be ok though. Obviously. A Pandemic will just bounce off him. He won't be doing smash and grabs from the local stores, and drinking a lot of reduced-price wine, that you can be sure of.

36

Fourth Day of Lockdown

9.45am

I wake up. I am getting later and later each day. Not by much. But a few minutes each day. Soon I will be waking up after high noon. And not even clearing up my kebabs and pot noodles from the day before. I am becoming an animal.

10.30am

I have been staring out my bedroom window for about the last five minutes. Makes me think of the office, somewhere out there. The building. Do buildings have souls? Is the office building weeping for its lifeblood, the actual office workers? No chatter through the offices, no one in the print room, no one in the lifts. I hope no one is in the lifts. Just deathly, eerie silences the length and breadth of the world.

I am in a tracksuit today. That feels like dressing up after having had my dressing gown on for most of the week. This is my new office attire. We aren't allowed to leave the house, so who cares about what anyone is wearing? I don't even have a pet to dress up for.

11am

There is another press conference from Boris and his scientific advisors, aka the political Bee Gees. These briefings are getting more gruesome by the day. The set-up is getting familiar now. Funny how you start to adapt and get used to new things like this. I am only ever looking for some movement in Boris's hair and tie. Boris looks like he may actually have straightened his tie (or paid someone to straighten it for him), but it seems like he has maybe just slightly over-straightened it today. Yes, he has. His tie is leaning the other way now. What is the man doing? I dig out the footage of his first lockdown speech on YouTube. This is something I didn't think I would be doing a week ago. Yes, I am correct, it was leaning to the left last week. Now, it's leaning to the right. How has he missed the fucking middle? His wardrobe department needs a bit of reshuffle.

11.10am

Boris has just left the stage. He mentions sixteen weeks today to crack this thing now. The timeframe is already being pushed back. It all sounds a bit non-committal though and panicky for my liking. Back to bed for an hour for me.

2pm

I wake up in a daze. I flick on my phone, trying to find anything that isn't related to the pandemic. I can't find anything.

Worryingly, thoughts turn to drink again. I don't want to end up like Oliver Reed, on some prime-time chat show, pissed and telling my life story. I'm not even a drinker. I may have been as a student, but with age, and more importantly parenthood, came at least some kind of responsibility. I have generally adhered to the chief medical officer's recommendations on unit intake per week. I think that it is now fourteen units for men. It used to be twenty-one units. Twenty years or so of being told that twenty-one units is all OK. Now suddenly it is fourteen units? Not an insignificant reduction. Someone should have handed in their badge and gun for that one. And as much as the government must have thought they were doing the right thing by announcing a reduction, they might not have considered the medical conditions flowing from the stress levels caused to a good percentage of the population who have now been told they have been abusing their liver for two decades. You have to hope the government's advice on health matters has tightened up, given that we are currently facing the greatest public health crisis for a generation.

37

Fifth Day of Lockdown

10am

My phone starts ringing. I'm just waking up. My phone is somewhere under the bed. Slipped down the crack again. Always down the crack. I can't find it. Where is that iPhone? Where is the slippery little window to the world? I get out of bed and stretch to get it. Something pulls slightly on my right side. Shit, that hurts. I need to warm up in the morning before stretching like this. That's what the pandemic is doing to me after just a week. Complete and total lack of fitness. Pulling muscles reaching for my phone. What's the meaning of a call at this time, anyway? Post-pandemic, 10am now equals about 7.50am pre-pandemic time.

It is an unknown number.

"Hello?" I say.

"Maxwell? Hiya, this is Dexter from work," says a completely unfamiliar voice.

"Hello," I say, still not properly awake.

"So, I am calling from office administration. We are just in the process of contacting as many employees as we can through various means. Management has tasked a few of us to carry out that role. First and foremost, how are you doing?" he says.

"Err, yes, not too bad, obviously in the circumstances," I reply, trying hard to sound like I have been awake for longer than two minutes.

"Good, that's good. That's the most important thing," Dexter carries on, with a noticeable lack of sincerity in his voice. Sounds like he is reading from a nicely prepared script. He is repeating words already. I think he has already run out of inspiration. This guy is no Charlie. Get Charlie to do the phone round. He would get everyone to believe he meant it.

"So Maxwell, the thing is we have had some discussions as to how we can keep the staff going remotely," he says. "We are in discussion with IT, and we will be arranging for laptops to be delivered to as many of us as we can. So we will also be e-mailing you with login codes for the systems, and a few other bits and bobs. Nothing too heavy at this stage. Just enough to keep you ticking over until we have a clearer picture as to what is going on," Dexter says.

"OK, thanks for the info," I say, not really registering what he's saying, or having the mental strength to ask a relevant question.

"OK, so any problems when you get all the kit through, just take it up with IT," he says.

No change there then.

"Oh, and just one other thing here is that you might want to try to source a quiet part of your house to maybe set up for a while. You know, desk and chair and all that."

"OK, thanks Dexter. Any idea when we will be back in the office?" I say, probably a tad naively.

"So not really at this stage. Just a bit of a waiting game, I think. It may be that we are in the eye of the storm at the moment. Hopefully we will come out the other end fairly soon. Take care in the meantime and be safe."

Oh dear Lord, even this guy Dexter from the office, whoever he is, is telling me to be safe now. This is like a horror film stuck on some kind of endless loop.

11am

I am sitting in the kitchen. Thoughts turn to food. I am getting a bit worried about the lack of food items in the house. There is nothing much in the cupboards. I am running low on milk, sugar, alcohol and all the other current essentials. I can't get online to order me anything. I am not a priority customer. The last time I logged in I was at number one million, five hundred and forty six in the queue.

I need to psych myself up for another trip to the local store. So far, the local store has been maintaining its stock levels. There is no panic buying yet. But the news is still grim. I don't want to go out. The government is introducing all these new rules. 'Social distancing' is the most prevalent. That is something to do with keeping about two metres from anyone else, to stop the pace of the spread of the virus. To be honest, I have probably been doing that for a little while in recent years already. Not sure how this two-metre rule is going to be enforced. Are we all going to be issued with a bamboo stick of two metres length, to be strapped to our foreheads?

2pm

After a warming pot noodle lunch, I start to think about what Dexter said. I haven't even thought about setting up an office at the house. I still think this is an elaborate joke, this whole Covid thing. Still the mother of all wind-ups. Every government in the world is in on it. But calls from people like Dexter is making this a bit more real. I need to seriously start thinking about how recreate an office set-up at home. There must be some advice on YouTube.

Wendy's house isn't large. It is a semi. There are a couple of spare rooms. But they are small. What I certainly don't have is any kind of operational, easy to slip into to when a lockdown hits, home office. But then who the fuck does? I point blank refuse to set up some kind of makeshift office in my bedroom. That would be taking me back to school. So actually, where am I going to set up this temporary office? It will have to be the small box room upstairs. There is an old desk in there. A small chair also. And it does have a window. I will need to look into that next week.

4pm

Ordinarily, this would be the start of the afternoon session. This is Friday. But no ordinary Friday – this is the Friday at the end of the first week of Armageddon.

I take out the whiskey bottle, grab an oversized pack of crisps, and watch TV in bed for the rest of the day. It is nearly the weekend, after all, lockdown or not. I don't do anything much different from that on a non-lockdown Friday. To be doing it at 4pm, though, is new.

38

Monday – Second Week of Lockdown

8.30am

My alarm goes off. That hasn't happened in years. Not a real one, anyway. I have been in bed for most of the weekend. My diet has been really poor and I have watched the first episode of pretty much every series currently on Netflix.

I am still in the design phase for the new home office. Still at the drawings stage. Nothing much else to do. I might as well try to do a proper job of it. I'm trying to visualise how I can turn the really small box room at the top of the house into a fully functioning office. I don't have any allocated budget to employ someone to design it. The current desk that is in there will probably do. It is a bit on the small side, and also a fraction on the shit side. I will need to wedge some books under one of the table legs. But it is all I have, so it will have to do. The chair is a little tricky. There is no other chair in anyone's house that is designed to be sat in all day long like a chair in the office is designed for. They are either too wooden, or too metal, or too much like a sofa. I will need to source an office chair. That will probably mean a weekend Ikea trip.

Maybe management is already on it. Bulk sourcing office chairs for us all. Somehow, though, the skeptic in me doubts we are all going to get any flatpack deliveries of office equipment any time soon.

10.30am

The doorbell rings. Who the fuck is that? We are in a pandemic. It is unlawful to socialise. This better not be the neighbourhood watch. Better be someone keeping their distance, adhering to the new social distancing guidelines. A visa or helmet over their respiratory system.

I open the door with a really cross face.

It is a delivery. My mood lightens slightly. Not one that I was aware of having ordered, however. There is a package on the floor, just outside my door. Ten yards or so back is the delivery man. He is masked up, bless his soul. But it is an odd look. It's like someone has just left a bomb on my doorstep, and he is the bomb disposal operator.

"I need a photo," the delivery man growls.

"Yes, no problem. Just make sure you get my good side," I reply. That particular attempt at humour is going down like a fart in a broken lift judging by the delivery man's total lack of reaction. I am holding the package and smiling like it is some kind of huge carp that I have just caught and the photographer is from the fishing channel. The delivery driver leaves. I don't think he did get my good side, to be honest. I don't have a good side anymore. Just pandemic face.

10.45am

Unwrapping the delivery. Ooh shit. It is from the office. Would you believe it? My lockdown laptop. Dexter has performed. God knows where management have dug these up from. There is no way they could have sourced these in bulk that quickly. They must have always had these in stock. Why the fuck has it taken a pandemic for laptops to be issued to all staff? It is beige though. Obviously.

11.42am

Just checking out the top 10 trending searches on Google. There it is again. It keeps coming up. Asteroid on a near collison course with the Earth. The top trending searches are a bit of a new thing. They are a bit of a barometer of the collective state of mind of the world. Since the pandemic has hit I think everyone is on high alert. Asteroids seem to the current flavour of the month. Tomorrow it will be a massive gingerbread man created by a chemical spill from a gingerbread factory just off the M42 on the rampage. A massive gingerbread man. Why not? Nothing is too insane now.

Lennox would call this worrying in the wrong place on a global scale.

11.45am

My new beige laptop is in its happy place. The charger is in its backside and is nearly fully juiced up. I am sat at my new desk, sat in my new workspace. I have tried to recreate the office scene as much as possible. But this is still very much makeshift.

I take in my new home working environment. The desk is the focal point, as it should be. The curtains are slightly stained; there's a bit of a fusty smell. Again, not too dissimilar to the office. I have ordered a lava lamp for my room though. Just to add a splash of colour. A bit like the office.

Here we go, I think, back in the office cockpit. I log on, sensationally remembering my password for once. Maybe it is because I haven't had any other information going round my brain for the last ten days or so. It takes a bit of time to get to my e-mails. Sure enough, it is the officewide IT e-mail that Dexter had been referring to. I am starting to get to like Dexter. This is a weird look though. Just the one blue e-mail in my inbox.

This IT e-mail is a long one. No problems with that at the moment. I have time to burn. Never used to be like that. Before lockdown I would have deleted these IT e-mails without reading. But I will consider this one carefully and leisurely, and with a cup of tea. It runs to a couple of pages. Here we go then. Long e-mails are true to form with IT. Always used to be. No reason to change now. Succinct is not a word in their vocabulary when it comes to e-mails. Anyway, having spent twenty minutes reading the e-mail, and then re-reading it again, I think the upshot of the e-mail is this:

1. You should all by now have received your laptops.
2. Your usernames and passwords for all applications are the same.
3. Stand by and await further instructions.

So no really useful bits then. Like when will we be back in the office? How are we going to run meetings and communicate with our office co-workers? And probably most fundamental of all, how am I going to fucking scan in or print out any stuff? I suppose I need to count my blessings. I am still in a job. And I haven't got Covid yet. It could all be far worse.

39

Tuesday – Second Week of Lockdown

8.50am

My suit is still hanging up from two weeks ago. It has been getting on my nerves for the last few days. It's like it has been taunting me. Just hanging there, goading me. I get up out of bed and walk over to it quite calmly and just in my boxer shorts, stop, and then just start dancing. Aggressively and with some venom. Maybe I am slightly losing the plot. Maybe I have lost it already. It is like I am releasing two weeks or so worth of pent-up energy, anger and emotion. I hope the neighbours haven't seen me. Not an easy one to explain away, that.

8.58am

After making my way downstairs, I enter my new coffee house. My kitchen. Suddenly I get a text from Noah. He must actually have my number stored in his phone. I didn't know he cared. Really quite an exciting moment for me this.

The text reads:

> *Hi Max how are you? The coffee house is shut for the moment obviously. But it isn't all bad. Am serving coffees to medical workers from a table in the back of my garden. See you soon my friend. Noah x*

I text him back:

> *Hi pal. Good on you. I suppose though this does mean no more flirting with the purple-haired girl for the moment for you. Ciao for now. Maxwell xx*

Noah texts back:

> *Oh no Maxwell, on the contrary my friend. I am virtual flirting all over the place at the moment. I will send you a link for a dating website. Get involved.*

9.30am

I'm a little late logging on. Usually at this time in the office, I would only just about have been finishing the obligatory round of 'Good morning's.

I didn't get many e-mails yesterday. Yesterday was all about logging on and checking my internet connection's stability, and that was about IP. So far my home internet connection is holding up. Applications seem to be loading OK for the moment. There are a handful of new e-mails over the weekend. About one an hour should take me to lunch. All the e-mails seem to be preceded by the now obligatory, 'Hope you are well", which is AKA "hope this little shit of a virus hasn't laid you out."

My desk doesn't look right. There is a laptop, mouse and charger. But the rest of the desk is bare. Where is all the stationery? The staples, pencils, rubbers, paperclips. The tools of the office workers trade. My desk is like a house with no paintings.

I need to improvise. I go on a search through my stuff in an old wardrobe. In amongst an old combination locked briefcase and some crusty socks I find my old pencil case from school. Unopened since probably about 1993. There could be anything in this. With a bit of trepidation I open it. There is a lot of dust, a lot of broken pens and pencils, and some glue. Then there is an old-style compass. You know, the ones with the very pointy ends. The ones that can take your eye out if you aren't concentrating. The ones that would most definitely not get past health and safety these days. A bit more of a rummage. Ah, there you go. A vintage fountain pen. What a specimen. A truly majestic-looking old-school pen. You can just imagine the office workers of days gone by, holed up in their dirty attics, with a pen like this, just hand-writing stuff. No computers in sight. No phones. No screens. Beautiful. For a second, the vision of this fountain pen takes me back to my youth. The nib is broken though, so I have to lob it in the bin.

I need to think about what I am going to need. Management needs to be doing stuff now also. There is more chance of Boris cutting a hairstyle than us getting back into the office any time soon. They need to be putting new policies in place to facilitate the brave new office world, and pretty fucking quickly.

40

Wednesday – Second Week of Lockdown

10.45am

After what seems like about forty-five minutes of staring out the window, I realise three-quarters of an hour has passed. Since I started work at ten, I have spent the last hour trying to work out what I need in terms of supplies. Homeworking equipment and the like. Stationery. I still can't find a pen (or pencil) anywhere in the house, which is bordering on a joke. So I have had to use an old pink highlighter pen for my list. The writing is big as a result, and the list stretches to two pages of A4. On the list is the following:

1. Pens.
2. Paper.
3. Staples and stapler.
4. Elastic bands.
5. Paperclips.
6. An office mug. Just generic. Or with a picture of a locked-down office worker on it.
7. A selection of biscuits in those two-biscuit

packets that you only ever get in office meeting rooms. You have those in the office. No reason not to have some at home.

8. A scanning and printing machine.
9. Printer paper.

This is not going to be an exhaustive list. This is a work in progress. This may stay in my draft e-mail folder for a little while yet.

2.15pm
Sat staring at my laptop. There have been a couple of spam e-mails since my lunch break. The kind of automatic computer-generated stuff that would still be sent out if the world was wiped out by a massive asteroid. Then the much-awaited further e-mail from Management arrives, with further instructions. It reads.

> *Dear all,*
>
> *As part of the transition phase to this new (albeit we hope temporary) way of working, we are aware that we must as far as possible maintain as many of the office procedures and policies as possible, and apply as many of those procedures to the new homeworking environment as possible. There will be several policies cascaded down over the next few weeks.*
>
> *This e-mail concerns health and safety issues, mainly as applied to your working environment.*

What exactly is my working environment? I think.

We are asking all staff to fill in a risk assessment, which will essentially take you through an analysis of your working space, to ensure the safety and comfort of staff during this period. We would ask staff to work through the attachment and complete this and return it to us as soon as possible.

OK, so what have we got here then? There are a series of questions.

1. Do you have a stable desk?

My reply: I have a desk but whether it is stable is another question entirely. The screws holding the legs together look like they might be a bit corroded.

2. Do you have a suitable chair?

My reply: I have a chair.

3. Does the work chair have a suitable and comfortable back that gives the lumbar region sufficient support, and keeps you in a predominantly upright position?

My reply: I have a chair.

4. Do you have adequate supplies and stationery?

My reply: Err, if you mean I have some old glue and a rubber from an old school pencil case that I found down the back of my wardrobe, then yes, I have adequate supplies. Otherwise, no.

5. Do you have any threats to your working environment, or any items on your desk that are dangerous or could cause you a headache?

My reply: I don't live in the best of neighbourhoods, so in terms of threats, I would probably put arson and burglary as a threat to my working pattern during normal office hours. In terms of items that could lead to headaches, lockdown hangovers may cause some headaches going forwards.

6. Do you have any specific needs or requirements?

My reply: I do certainly but this might not be the right forum to air them publicly.

I delete before sending. I am not replying to this. It doesn't take anyone any further forward.

I knock off for the day.

41

Tuesday – Third Week of Lockdown

I am in my lockdown pyjamas today. I don't have the energy to change. You would have thought I would have enough energy given all the sleep I am getting. But I don't. I have even spent some of the early part of the day partially nude from the waist down, before affording myself the self-dignity of putting my PJ's on. I have a few other lockdown outfits. The main one is a nice silk khaki gown, decorated with koi carp. I may get it out for the weekend. But there are some outfits that are so loud and lairy that you don't feel you can wear them even behind closed doors. The koi carp may be one of them. So I might need a Friday night triple brandy before I have the gumption to put it on. Tony the cyclist wouldn't have that issue though. He would probably change into this after his bike ride. And probably exit the office showers with it on. Probably open. As long as he doesn't forget his work trousers. I smile, remembering the incident. It is the little things you miss…

Is this what it feels like to be retired? No need to get suited and booted. No need to shave. No need to prepare an outfit for each day of the week. Nothing to do but maybe walk the dog. Or just go for a walk if you don't have a dog. Catch up with some friends over lunch and gorge on cheese and wine. All very civilised. Finally get round to watching the second episodes of all the Netflix series that you have started, trying in the process to remember what the hell went on in the first episode. Or even read a newspaper. Not your phone. An actual newspaper that you hold in your hands. The ones that cost £5 and then when you get home you realise all the supplements have fallen out.

12pm

My office lockdown lunchtime hours have now become 12–2pm. So time to have a break from staring out the window and have some lunch. I have been moving to this new earlier lunchtime over the last week or so. I am not sure that it is aligned with any official Management-ratified policy, but this is my house (well, Wendy's) and my rules. So Management can fucking spin if they don't like the new office hours. Start time is now also 10am. Moved from 9.30am earlier in the week.

Lunch

I'm in my kitchen currently. It is about 12.03, not that time really matters anymore. I pour myself a cup of tea and it occurs to me that for the first time in my office life, I can make a drink without pressure. I find myself actually watching the kettle boil. Without the pressure of getting a round in for a fellow office worker. None of these mugs fall into any categories. There is no current threat of abuse from inadvertently using a category 3 mug. All the mugs in this kitchen are mine. Or Wendy's. This is all different. Some of this isn't completely all bad. For lunch I see what I have in the fridge. Food is weighing on my mind though. On an initial perusal, I have a few packets of cheese, three loaves of bread, some beetroot and some old ham in my fridge. I am starting to think like we are already on rations. It may not be long before we truly are. It won't be long before I have to do the first major foray out of my house to the supermarket. I need more than my local shop now. My local's supplies are starting to run low.

For now though, I have just about enough for a sandwich. It wont be much to write home about. In the freezer I do have some chicken nuggets, but that is for the weekend. It wouldn't feel right to whack chicken nuggets and chips into the oven at 1pm on a Tuesday. I'm not oven cooking at lunchtime. That won't be happening. That would be like having a glass of wine on a Monday morning. The only time that is acceptable for anyone who is not an alcoholic would be in the departure lounge at an airport. That said, I have come close to a glass of wine at 6am in the last couple of weeks.

2pm

After my extended lunch I am back in my office and find myself staring out the window again. Not really thinking about much. Just staring at the sky. I have spent a lot of time staring at the sky over the last few weeks.

185

There hasn't been much else to do. I hadn't realised how much stuff goes on in the sky before now. It's a whole separate world. When does anyone have any time to look up? Apart from when a pandemic hits, that is. But at any one time, an awful lot of stuff goes on in the sky. Hot air balloons, aeroplanes, aeroplane vapour trails, helicopters, people skydiving, the moon, Jupiter, Uranus. And maybe if you squint really hard, and couple that with really high-powered binoculars, you might see Elon Musk trying to buy some land on Mars to build a hotel.

If we ever do get through this pandemic, there should be a major design change in offices, universities, schools, YMCAs the world over. There should be an atrium-style window in the ceiling with a motorised recliner seat. It should be every office worker's right from now to take a break when they need to, to sit back, look up and take in whatever might be going on in the sky at that point.

That's going to be the new thing. There is a lot of looking down. Looking sideways. But not much looking up. It takes me back for a moment to the day of my fall outside the coffee shop. That was enforced. Where Noah hadn't properly gritted his exit. But I am going to make sure that I take more time to look up in the future. Yes sir.

And maybe one day I will finally work out what happens to helium balloons …

42

Wednesday – Third Week of Lockdown

12pm

We're well into the third week of lockdown now. I have another slightly more leisurely, chilled morning. Each day just sightly less panic, a little more calm. Just slightly. That said, that might be partly because of my self-imposed social media blackout. It has taken a pandemic for me to reduce my reliance on my phone. I don't want actual news at the minute. That's been my decision for a little while. I don't want real-time social media. I don't want someone else's take on how bad it is. I know how bad it is out there. You can feel it. Everyone can feel it. It is all around. Even without reading about it. Collective silence is the only news headline out there. I have also decided against getting into newspapers. It might have been a nice idea but that boat has long since sailed.

But in my own little lockdown bubble, I have started to feel a change. I might just very, very slowly be starting to get used to it. There may even be, amongst all this undiluted chaos going on… there might actually be… well, maybe there is actually something to this homeworking idea. Just slightly. Just ever so slightly. If that is even possible.

Adhering as I am to the new laws of curfew and lockdown, I haven't been out the house for at least two weeks now, apart from trips to store for my 'essentials'. Other concerns are surfacing though. For example, I am starting to get just a little bothered about food. I haven't much cheese and bread left. Or toilet paper. My shop has run out of them. The ham that I have been making for my lunch every day is starting to curl up at the sides and go hard. Much longer and that ham will be doing damage to my teeth. And with dentists – like everyone else at the moment – sat at home, playing cards or extended games of Monopoly, damage to my teeth is the last thing I want.

The milkman has been my lifeline for dairy produce. He is still delivering, God bless him. I suppose that is one job that can carry on during a pandemic. There's not much risk of catching this virus at 2am when you are on a milk float on your own. He is a bit like the tooth fairy. I don't think I have ever seen him. I do hear him though. He seems to enjoy flooring his supercharged milk float at about 2.30am every morning. Just to help with my current pandemic-induced insomnia.

12pm
There is a little more movement on the e-mails today. Each day it seems office workers are slowly but surely starting to emerge from their bunkers, drink in some daylight, and maybe just try to start their commercial engines again.

Mine needs a bit of an oil change. But I am trying at least. As long as you are in the game, you are still potentially winning. Another one of Noah's, I believe.

That said, I don't think anyone is expecting any real productivity. I mean productivity and output is now all relative. Relative to the mother of all human problems hitting not more than three weeks ago. No one is expecting pre-pandemic output. This is like learning how to walk again.

I feel for Management at the moment. They are all human, after all. All with their own problems, their own insecurities, their own domestic set-ups. Maybe I have been too harsh on them. Can anyone really steer a commercial ship in this storm? Maybe they don't give two shits just at the moment. They are probably all still dribbling in fear on their bathroom floors, letting IT deal with all the important stuff for the moment, and calling for their mums.

8pm Clapping

I am currently stood on Wendy's lawn. Clapping. Clapping for the medical workers. This was suggested as a good thing to do by the government. I think this is one thing we don't need to be told to do. I get it. I think people get it. We get that the people on the frontline of this bullshit is where the best of human resilience currently lives. Medical people. Nurses, doctors, scientists. People getting supplies to people.

The human network. A very powerful thing when tested.

I have no idea how medical people deal with this

stuff. I can't handle medical things. I never wanted to know the inner workings of my body. I don't even get the outer workings. Take surgeons. Geniuses. Life-changing people. But on a day-to-day level, how you can take someone's liver out just before breaking for lunch and a corned beef sandwich and salad is beyond me. I knew from an early age that my career destiny was not in healthcare.

I started clapping about a minute ago. I'm standing in Wendy's overgrown garden, in the dark, clapping. Just three weeks ago I would have been given an asbo for doing this. It felt a bit weird at first. Just a solitary clap from someone down the road. But the pace is now building and we are properly riding the clapping equivalent of this street's Mexican wave. Clapping and giving the bird to Covid at the same time. I think I may have just let out a whoop also a second ago. There is a guy down the road with a steel drum. That might be taking it a bit far.

43

Thursday – Third Week of Lockdown

6.20am

My phone is vibrating on my bedside cabinet. It is a text from Wendy.

A text at 6.20am from Wendy. She can't be trying to wake me up from two hundred miles away? Surely?

It reads:

Maxxie, sorry to let you know this over text but my Dad died yesterday. I need to stay here for a bit and sort stuff out/look after my mum. Speak soon x

Ah no, I thought he was on the mend. I liked her dad. We got on. He liked a drink and a laugh. To be fair it was probably the drink that killed him. I hope it wasn't this virus. He probably didn't regret a moment though. Hope Wendy is OK.

Awful, Wendy. Really sorry. No words. Let me know if you need anything. Love Maxwell xx

1pm

I decide to do some gardening. Wendy would expect me to make sure her house was kept well. I owe it to her. The garden is small and a bit overgrown. Mainly my fault. I think Wendy has given me further mate's rate discount on account of me mowing the lawn and keeping it nice and tidy. I haven't quite kept to that side of the bargain. Maybe this is my time to address that, even though gardening isn't my specialism. I can't let Wendy's garden go to shit. It will never be the Chelsea flower show, but it should be better than the garden next door. Everyone's garden should be better than the one next door. I might feel a bit better too. Get some sun on my face. Get the heart turning over again. It is early spring, and the weather is actually pretty good for this time of year. I might even get a dose of Vitamin D from the sun. Apparently that might be good for the immune system. And what is good for the immune system is bad for Covid.

There is a tiny shed in the back garden. You couldn't really call it a shed to be fair. More of a hobbit's toilet. All it houses is the smallest lawnmower known to man and an old electric hedge cutter. I brush off the cobwebs from the electric hedge cutter and power it up.

The hedge at the back of the house needs a bit of work. It has taken a worldwide pandemic to get me to the point where I am holding this hedge cutter in my hands. Now that it is on, I am not too sure how to use it. I am looking at it oscillating in my hands, and then looking left and right to see if anyone can see me staring at it. I am suddenly very self-conscious. This is a pandemic and I am holding what looks a bit like a chainsaw in my hands, just staring at it. I think I may also still have my dressing gown on. The neighbourhood WhatsApp group must be nearly calling 999 by now.

So do I go clockwise or anticlockwise to trim my bush? Fuck it, here goes. It doesn't go through smoothly. There seems to be a lot of kickback. Twigs are flying around. Then there is a slightly gurgling noise and a small plume of smoke, and then silence. I have cut through the wire to the hedge cutter. I leave it on the ground and run inside.

44

End of Fourth Week of Lockdown

Friday, 8pm

I am in bed at the end of the fourth week of lockdown. I am just lying there, staring at the ceiling. Not the sky this time. Not out the window. I don't feel like it at the moment. So I am currently just staring at the ceiling. I am still upset about Wendy's dad. She will be in pieces. They were close.

And I am thinking about Covid. In all the panic, I don't think I have actually addressed my mind to this thing. The bigger picture and all that. Where is this thing going to end? Will it end? Is the world now split into two ages, before Covid and after Covid? What part does religion play in all this? Is religion the answer? Is science the answer?

And also – am I what is known as a keyworker? 'Keyworker' is a new term that the government has introduced. That is, people working in professions who are basically essential to fighting the virus and keeping the country fed, as far as I can tell.

So where do I sit in all this? Where do my fellow

office workers sit in a debate of usefulness? If the medical community is at the top of the tree, and say, wrestlers (no disrespect intended), are about a thousandth on the list, where do we fit in? Top ten, top fifty? Do we even make the top hundred? Office worker is a broad category. Medical worker is narrower. Medical worker, somewhere along the line, has to do with the human body. But office worker? What are we? What is an office worker really? An office worker could be an accountant working in a hospital? And actually, maybe I was too hasty with wrestling. Wrestling is entertainment. People need to be entertained. So are the entertainers who are entertaining the keyworkers, themselves keyworkers? What about the wardrobe department for the wrestlers that keep the wrestlers going, and keep the keyworkers entertained?

I end with the realisation that I, Maxwell Orwellian, am not in any way, shape or form a keyworker. But I am still higher in the pecking order than Daniel. That may have to do. A small victory. I need to feel some self-worth. I am higher than Daniel, aren't I?

8.30pm
Boris and the advisers are doing a late evening Covid update. I have watched most of these since after the first week of lockdown with no sound. I am just waiting for the day that Boris's hair doesn't look like he has just hatched five chicks out of it. I think that will be the day when humankind has defeated this virus. That must be the day that Covid admits defeat, packs its bags and fucks back off to where it came from. China or some lab somewhere. That is the sign in my mind, anyway.

Boris's hair. There may not be much logic to it. But there isn't much logic behind Covid either. So two can play that game.

I am not sure why, but I decide to check in on the news today. With some volume. This is dangerous. I haven't done this for a while. I have pretty much self-imposed a social media ban on myself since the second week of lockdown. I have reduced my phone plan down to help with reducing the reliance on my phone, and thus the temptation to get drawn into social media. I previously had unlimited data. I am now on the old internet equivalent of pay as you go.

Today I demand inspiration from Boris. Or if not inspiration, then at least a load of lies to try to make us all feel better. I reckon at this stage the government's job is not to encourage but to bullshit, tell us some lies. Tell us the sun isn't about to blow up even if it is. That's what we need. The people demand dishonesty. And we demand it now. It is out democratic right. I might form a band with the man with the steel drum on the street. Get the message out. May even form a new political party. The Bullshit Party, I will call it. It will immediately make you feel better. Boris is probably as much in the dark as anyone. He is probably on the phone with his mum most of the time.

Boris looks panicky. Far from tranquil. Physically a bit dishevelled, as usual. He is falling between two stools. He looks better than Winston Churchill did, but he sounds worse. Maybe next time he should be on a horse, with thirteenth-century warpaint on. Boris the Braveheart. Seems unlikely though. His hair can't be tamed. On that realisation I go back to sleep for a while, safe in the knowledge that in about four hours I will be plagued by another unexplainable lockdown dream…

45

End of the Fifth Week of Lockdown

Friday, 8.30pm

Not much of any note happened just this last week. I am starting to enjoy my early Friday evening contemplations in bed. I call this my 'ceiling time'. That said, my outfits have changed a bit over the course of the last week. I seem to have progressed from pyjamas, to nude from the waist down, to grey tracksuit bottoms. I have a shirt on today though. Not sure why. I just feel like it today. It's like a halfway house. Not at home. But not in the office. Hybrid. A hybrid office worker.

Time, though. That's becoming the enemy at the moment. I have loads of it. Too much of it. Filling time in the day is a challenge at the moment. In the days. In the evenings. Due to my natural restless office worker syndrome, I have decided to change tack on the home entertainment front. I have spent a bit of time working out how many films and series I have access to based on the eleven film apps on my TV. That is currently 102,545 films and 43,345 series. That killed a bit of time. No wonder I can't get past the third episode of any series. How can anyone ever find anything to watch with that much choice?

Saturday, 6.50pm

I am sat there looking at a dating app that Noah has sent me. Rocking back and forth on the kitchen chair in the kitchen. Surely it hasn't yet come to this. Surely it hasn't taken a pandemic to push me to this point. Online dating. I have been thinking about it all night. Couldn't really sleep thinking about it. Tossing and turning again. Going through the pros and cons in my mind. I have only ever really been with my wife since meeting all those years ago in the sweet shop. I don't think I had even spoken to a girl before then. I am not sure I have since.

So having realised the pros may just ever so slightly outweigh the cons, I quickly drink a small wine that I poured about an hour ago and, having decided to take the plunge, I click the link. There is no going back.

To register I have to upload ten photos – five head shots and five full frontals. And you need to basically write an essay about yourself. I wasn't expecting this level of detail. I thought a dating website was just one passport-like photo and your age. Jesus, how wrong could I be. This thing tries to match you on every level. Physical, emotional, spiritual. Even your political allegiances. I might not put down that I want to see Boris on a horse, or that I am the new leader of the Bullshit Party. That stuff might scare people off. My standards for a prospective partner are currently quite low. I don't want to date Noah or anyone who looks like me. That's all. I don't think that is too much to ask.

7.45pm

Two more glasses of wine down and about halfway through the compatibility questionnaire. This is going to be a long night…

46

Start of Sixth Week of Lockdown

Monday, 2.30pm

This afternoon, after doing nothing particularly this morning, I have tried to take some baby steps back into some kind of work normalcy. I have – very, very briefly – thought about putting on a tie. I haven't yet. I have caught up on a few e-mails I have been storing up. There have only been seven the whole week so it didn't take me long. Usually, e-mails in pre-Covid days were a little bit like playing a game of tennis. Get the ball (e-mail) back in the other person's court as quickly as possible. It was all about keeping your current unread e-mails under about twenty to thirty. Anything more than that and you were in the red zone. But not in this new lockdown world. No one would give a shit if it took you three days to reply to an e-mail. I think people just want to know they are not alone.

There have been a few more e-mails from IT. The usual generic stuff. Not really advancing anyone's understanding of what we are supposed to be doing at home. 'Working environments' keeps being mentioned. Still not quite sure what that means.

Management has started to emerge a little from the shadows though. They have sent a few e-mails about 'taking their lead from the government as to the next steps'. That kind of stuff. So they are still on their phone to their mums. Hopefully, though, the conversations are just getting a little bit shorter now.

My alcohol intake went up massively over the weekend. I had got it a little under control after the first two or three weeks of lockdown. That was panic drinking. But the wheels of restraint loosened a bit on Saturday whilst answering the questions about my personality on the dating website, and then fully came off. I ended up lying down in the garden yesterday looking up at the stars and singing My Way by Frank Sinatra. The neighbours must now be thinking I have suffered a lockdown emotional breakdown.

I am sat in my kitchen. I have my mobile banking app up. Thoughts have turned to financial issues. Today is usually pay day. But do we still get paid in a pandemic? Is Jim from Accounts even working? Who pays Jim from Accounts? I don't even know how I get paid. How do people get paid? Is it automatic? Do I get paid even though I have done basically fuck-all in the last month? More questions than answers. But so far the balance is showing as £9. That is what is left, not my monthly salary. So I think that must mean I haven't been paid yet. I will refresh this later and see whether I need to kill myself or not. I now check my sent text items. Always a worry on the day after a bender. Ten texts sent. A few to Wendy, a few to Noah (now that I have his mobile). A lot of thumbs up and kisses. A couple that were undeliverable. Nothing too bad. No responses yet from anyone.

Tuesday, 12.36am

I have been asleep, surprisingly for around a couple of hours. And for once, no sheep were hurt in the process. Suddenly something wakes me up. A faint smell of burning. No, a really strong smell of burning. Really strong. I get up quickly. Why has the smoke alarm not gone off? Then I remember there are no smoke alarms in this house. Shit. Where is it coming from? I tear at the curtains, half asleep, half in real panic mode. I look out the window. Holy Mother of God, the neighbour's garage on the other side of the street is on fire. Not a smouldering fire. A proper, full on fire. With smoke and flames and everything.

I think it is an elderly couple that live there. I just react. I don't need the office fire wardens. I don't need my high-vis jacket. I am on auto-pilot already. I would like to say training is kicking in. But I haven't ever had any training. So it can't be that.

Still in my slightly stained lockdown pyjamas, I run down the stairs and out the house. Shit, it is even worse up close. The garage is separate from the main house but it looks like there is a car in it. Any petrol in that engine and we could be kissing goodbye to the whole street in a crescendo of steel drums and shrapnel.

I scream at the window of the house. They are elderly. They are unlikely to be out at an all-night rave in lockdown. No reply. This is now very dangerous.

203

There is a lot of heat coming from the garage. And there is a car in there. The old boy likes vintage cars. There is definitely a potentially flammable vintage car in there. Fucking around in his garage I wouldn't be surprised is what has probably caused this fire in the first place.

I keep screaming at the bedroom window of the house. For fuck's sake, get up. How can they not see and hear this? Where's the guy with the steel drum when you need him?

Suddenly the bedroom light is switched on. The man pops his head out and looks at me. I am pointing furiously to his garage. He keeps looking at me. How can he not see the massive ball of smoke ten metres to his right. He is now waving at me. I think he thinks I am waving. Why the fuck would I be waving at him in the middle of the night? Seriously, why? *You are going to die if you don't get a grip.*

Suddenly it dawns on him. I can hear him shouting something to his wife. 'Get out, there is a fire!' would be an option in the circumstances. The front door opens and he bolts out the door in dressing gown and slippers. Towards the garage. Towards a garage with the roof on fire. There is a slight pause. Suddenly I can hear an engine going on, a screech of tyres. Out of the flaming garage comes his vintage car. This guy is insane. Has he got a deathwish?

1.15am

Finally the fire brigade arrive. They deal with the roof. Proper keyworkers dealing with real shit. Great scenes in the end. Obviously the whole road comes out, as people always do when a house is on fire on the street, lockdown or no lockdown. I go back to bed.

1.35am

The door bell goes. You are kidding. I was nearly asleep then, which doesn't happen very often. I am on a tiredness-induced war path as I put my koi carp dressing gown on and make my way downstairs.

I open the door. It is the elderly lady from opposite. The one whose life I have just saved.

"Hello, love," she says.

She takes a step inside the house. Without a mask. "I just wanted to say thank you so much for waking myself and Leonard up. We hadn't heard anything."

Really shows how people on this street look after each other," she says.

"OK, thanks, and no problem. Anyone would have done the same, obviously," I say.

I suddenly realise she is in my house though, closer than two metres to me and without a mask.

I feel slightly enraged by this.

"Sorry, can I just ask you to step back?" I say.

"Sorry love, step back? How do you mean?" she says.

As well as not realising their garage was on fire, this couple are clearly unaware that there is a pandemic going on.

She suddenly realises.

"Oh sorry love, yes sorry. Just am a bit flustered after everything that has just happened. Anyway thanks so much again."

She leaves. I worry for her. Her husband is obviously more concerned about his vintage car than his, or his wife's, wellbeing.

I go back to bed, emotionally and physically a bit fucked from the last hour or so. This has played havoc with my insomnia. I might aswell just pull a chair up though and sit by the door. It seems like the night for people to keep knocking.

47

Wednesday – Sixth Week of Lockdown

9.30am

I need to try to continue to count my blessings. However fragile my mental state might be, might yet become, I still haven't had Covid and my garage, if I had one, isn't yet on fire.

And also, although Wendy's house is not the biggest in the world, I don't live in a high-rise block of flats. I have a garden. Admittedly overgrown. And with the hedge cutter wire still severed and no shops or electricians available to mend it, it looks like that situation might continue for a while yet. But it is a garden nonetheless.

I also don't have to commute to the office or need to wear a suit and tie. Does that make me feel like less of an office worker? Possibly. But that also means less time spent in the evenings getting ready for the following office day. So I have more time to watch YouTube and maybe one day actually devote enough time to finding something to watch on Netflix.

And what of the office? Again, got to take some positives. Not having to bump into Jim from Accounts.

Not having to listen to Dan's narcissistic, self-unaware rants. Being able to sample a range of mugs from the kitchen without the fear of the threat of violence.

11.05am

I have spent the last couple of hours drawing. I have ended up drawing a 3D picture of a table. I was trying to remember if I knew how to do it. Evie taught me that when she was about eight. And I hadn't tried to draw it again until now. I remembered. I have had some texts from Evie. More than in a long while. More positives...

My desk is still fairly clean. I spray anti-bacterial spray on the desk at the end of each day, given that there are no cleaners in this house. I have bulk bought Dettol spray. It is all over the house. Empty cans litter the place. The paint around the door handles is all stripped off from where I have been spraying them. What I haven't really thought through is that I live on my own, so disinfecting the house isn't really necessary.

But I am adhering well to my own clean-desk policy in my office. Mainly because I still have nothing to put on it. Just the stapler I had from school in the top left-hand corner. I think there might be the beginnings of a cobweb on it. I straighten it slightly. It isn't quite parallel to the left-hand edge of my desk. No, actually, tell a lie. The left-hand edge of the desk isn't straight. I turn it back.

Oh holy Lord above, today there is a major follow up e-mail from Management just landed. This is very exciting. I never thought I would ever say that.

Dear all,

First and foremost, and I appreciate it probably does go without saying, but I hope all of you, our valued and loyal staff, are keeping well. These are quite extraordinary, unprecedented times that we all find ourselves currently living through.

We have all needed time to draw breath and to take stock of the situation. There is a benefit at times to standing back and assessing as much of a situation as is possible before making any decisions on the appropriate way forward.

The current advice from the government is that as far as we can, employees and staff should be working from home. We are all of course physically based at home and you will by now all have a series of e-mails from IT, who have been tasked with managing the transition of staff to be able to work from home. You will appreciate this is a huge task and we are still in the early stages so you will need to bear with us, but I do hope you appreciate we are still taking our lead from the government.

What is clear is that we will be in this phase for the foreseeable future. So to that end, we are asking staff as much as possible to start the process of getting back into the working routine. Once the systems to enable home-working are fully in place, we should be able to return to some form of a working structure.

We should also be rolling out communications systems through several software platforms that will allow you to communicate with colleagues.

Dialogue and communication within and across teams is obviously is very important, especially now. Not just in a work context but also on a personal level. We are all social beings, we need one another.

Not strictly true across the board for me. I am enjoying having a break from Daniel.

So to summarise, please first, and most importantly, take care of yourselves, but you should all be capable over the next few days of returning to at least some semblance of normality concerning working patterns. We will be suspending, in the circumstances, some of our key output targets for staff, but we hope to be able to re-introduce those soon.
Take care in the meantime.

That e-mail, if translated into normal language, could have been shorter. More along the following lines:

Dear all,
We do not have a Scooby-Doo as to what is going on. The company could be a goner in less than two weeks. To avoid that scenario you have had a couple of weeks dossing but you need to get back to work right now to keep this company above water and keep food on your tables.
Best wishes.

Suspending office targets. Again, in my office lifetime that has never happened. That probably makes sense. But how is the company going to pay staff? There is some government support going on. Some credits, tax breaks. Talk of the government paying people's salaries. Maybe that is what it is all about.

Half of us could be out of a job in two weeks. The lucky other half would still be employed but would be struggling to keep up mortgage payments due to the extra heating costs. This is just a revolving door of worry. One worry gets off, and another gets in. Where's Lennox?

I fall off the wagon again. I need a drink.

48

Wednesday of the Seventh Week of Lockdown

12pm

People are now wearing masks across the board. Not out of choice either. We are being ordered to cover our faces and noses with masks whenever we go shopping or mix with anyone other than people we live with. The police are enforcing this.

I can see that armed robbery could be a problem. How are the police supposed to spot the armed robbers from decent law-abiding shoppers now? That distinction used to be clear. Generally people going into shops with bad intent generally wore something over their face so you couldn't identify them. Like a bike helmet or a balaclava. Average shoppers intending on paying for their shopping, wouldn't be wearing stuff over their face. From today, it will now be encouraged to go shopping with a balaclava and a helmet.

I don't yet have a mask, so I am not quite sure how I can adhere to the policy of wearing a mask in the shop.

I assume that you are allowed to drive to a shop with the specific intention of buying a mask, but that you can't go anywhere else.

To make matters worse, I have now completely run out of food. The cheese and beetroot went long ago. The ham hardened and reduced in size. My milkman has gone off grid.

It isn't just food either. I need some razors and now all my socks now have holes in them from the wear and tear of my pacing up and down for hours. I need to brave the outside world. I still haven't been able to secure any online deliveries. I seem to be further back in the queue for an online delivery than ever. The whole world is trying to ship their food in. Panic buying has all gone online.

Anyway, I write a little shopping list of stuff, get in my car, which still has nearly a full tank as I haven't been out in two months, take some deep long breaths, say a little prayer and make my way to the shop.

Seven weeks ago, if I had told myself that I would be shitting myself on the way to a shopping trip to the supermarket, I would have assumed that would be because I had eaten an undercooked sausage, not for fear of getting killed by a virus.

12.22pm

I arrive at the supermarket in my car. I have an all-in-one tracksuit on. A bit like a onesie. But I don't care about any of that now. This isn't a fashion show. No one gives two shits what anyone looks like at the moment. This is about getting as much as I need out of this shopping trip and getting back to the safety of my house.

I switch the engine off and survey the scene. I have packed a pair of pocket binoculars. I acquired them from a theatre trip years ago. You know, the type that is attached to the back of the seat in front of you. I thought they were complimentary but found out some time later that that wasn't the case.

I don't need the binoculars, though, to see that there is a massive queue. People queuing to get into my local supermarket. Not a small affair either. It is like a civil rights movement but without any noise or placards. A one in, one out policy. And people spaced out. I mean spaced out physically from each other in the queue, but also probably a good proportion of them spaced out mentally, either from chemicals or from stress. If I had a megaphone this might be a great place to garner support for the newly formed Bullshit Party.

I pan left and right through the theatre binoculars. I am not quite sure what else I am looking for though. Everything else seems normal. But where is the trolley park? Yes, OK, so I see it now. About ten metres from the back of the queue. OK, I have my bearings. I also have my shopping list. Usually, I would keep taking the list out in the store, but I imagine that kind of dawdling will be frowned upon at the minute and would probably get me ejected from the store, so I have spent some of my morning office time memorising the shopping list. I give myself a quick memory refresh. This is a new list. This is a list for a new mid- pandemic, post-apocalypse type world with a bit of a new homeworking vibe. There is a lot more toilet paper and wine on it.

12.27pm

After a final shopping list recap, I start to make my way to the trolley park. So far so good; there is no one yet within two metres of my airspace. I pick up the pace slightly. The advice is that this virus can be transmitted on surfaces, and in particular metal surfaces. The trolley handle therefore could be a breeding ground. I have some boiling water to chuck over the trolley. The issue I hadn't quite contemplated is that the water wouldn't be hot when I got to the store. So its virus destruction qualities may not be what I would hope.

However, it is all that I have. So I chuck some lukewarm water over the handle.

"Hey mate," someone says from behind me.

Is he talking to me? This is weird. If he is, I am not sure I can remember how to hold a conversation.

"Yes," I say.

"There is some trolley sanitiser over there, pal," he says, pointing to some trolley sanitiser.

I will know for future. I make my way to the back of the queue.

12.29pm

This is a very strange experience. I am at the back of a queue at my local supermarket, with people in single file, two metres from the next person, some with masks on and with no one talking to each other.

12.59pm

I am still in the queue. A bit nearer to the front but not by much.

1.05pm

Am finally at the entrance of the store. There is a high-vis-wearing security guard at the door. He is monitoring the number of people in the store I assume. He beckons me in. My concern about the mask is slightly resolved. There is a pack of them on the way in. Not sure how hygienic it is though. Hands in the same pack of masks. Nevertheless, putting one of these on is the only way I am going to be able to put food on the table tonight.

This store is usually rammed with people, weekday or weekend. But there seems to be no one around, at least not in the first section of the store, which is the vegetable section. Am I the only one in here? Is this an episode of Supermarket Sweep? Either way, I feel a slight pang of satisfaction. Maybe this is as it should be? No-one breathing down your neck when you are buying an aubergine. I don't hang around in the fruit and veg section though. This is no time to be healthy.

As I move through the store there are slightly more people. Everyone must have had the same idea about the fruit and veg section. There are more people, it seems, in the pasta section, the discounted microwave food section, and the biscuit, crips and sweets aisles. Oh, and the booze aisle, of course. That is rammed.

But before I can get into any of that, I need to get some masks. I am going to need a few packs.

1.07pm

I am in the mask aisle. The mask aisle is a temporary stand shoehorned into the stationery and office supplies section of the store, just behind the party aisle.

I have never bought a mask before. What am I even looking for? There are loads of them. Unhelpfully, they are also mixed in, it seems, with the party masks. Which idiot thought that that was a good idea? There are loads of different colours, designs, themes. Superheroes, horror films, fluorescent colours. I just need a basic mask. I need something that suits my mood, and possibly suits a return to the office in due course. Found them. There is a pack of plain shit brown ones right at the end of the aisle. I take five packets.

1.09pm

I decided a week or so ago that I am not going to wait for Management to send through office supplies. I think they are all spent after organising the supply of home laptops. I need to take the initiative. So I am going to get all the tools of my trade from here. In my local supermarket, of all places. I will be keeping an itemised receipt and will be sending that and an invoice to the office.

So what do I need? Pens, pencils, envelopes (all sizes and colours; some with windows, some without), some glue, staples, a heavy-duty stapler, notepad. Some nice scented candles. Tea, coffee.

Then there is the new home office wear. Pyjamas, slippers, maybe a smoking jacket and pipe. To add to my silk koi carp dressing gown.

All going on expenses.

1.15 pm

In amongst all of the rice, beans, socks and razors is a load of office stuff. I don't know whether this has always been here or whether I am just now focused on it. Who cares? I lob in a printer and some printer paper to my trolley. Jim from Accounts will have a breakdown when he sees the price tag for that.

There is some form of arrow system on the floor. Yellow arrows. All pointing the way. The kind of thing that they have backstage at concerts or the theatre, directing the stars to the stage. It is like a pedestrian one-way system, put together to help shoppers socially distance themselves. I am trying to follow this one-way system but it is not giving me the most efficient route to the stuff I need. It looks like some people in the store are adhering to this new system and some aren't. I am at least trying to toe the line.

I am now in the booze section. There are more people to avoid here. One chap is getting way too close to me. He is ignoring my new two-metre airspace exclusion zone. I move slightly forward. He follows. I can almost feel his breath on the back of my neck. This is my new, government-backed right for him not to be near me. Is he taking the piss? Is he one of those evil people trying to infect others? Biological warfare in my local supermarket. I should have made that homemade two-metre bamboo stick strap-on device. You better not cough. I do a quick time check. I have eaten into my new two-hour lockdown lunchtime. I like to watch a bit of telly before starting the afternoon sessions. Also, I think I may have seen Jim from Accounts in the world foods section. Might have been wrong. May have been my mind playing tricks on me. I am not running the risk though. I pay on self-service after scanning my stuff, wash my hands in the bog, and make my way home. Back to safety.

218

49

Thursday – Seventh Week of Lockdown

The Crystal Ballroom

3pm

There is a new global e-mail from IT. It is headed 'Communications policy going forward'.

> *Dear staff,*
>
> *Further to the e-mail from Management last week, we have now developed the platform that we all need to be using for both internal and external communications going forwards.*
>
> *The link below will take you to the sign-in page for the software, the process for installing the app, and your username/ID.*
>
> *Any problems, please speak to a member of IT.*

I click on the link. As usual with IT e-mails, the links take you to some strange places. I like the links that just allow you to click through them without any thought.

But this link opens up a Word document. A Word document with about twelve instructions for how to install the video conferencing, followed by security measures and so on and so forth. Ordinarily, in the hustle and bustle of a busy non-lockdown day in the office, pre-pandemic, this would be another example of an IT e-mail that would be right clicked and deleted, possibly without reading. But again, in the more relaxed pace and vibe of locked-down office working, averaging around twenty-three minutes per day of actual output-generating work, and with current performance targets pretty much scrapped, this is all OK. I can invest some time in this.

Not just yet though. First I want to finish watching a podcast that I started later last night lying in bed. It is all about digestion. It is called the 'The silent assassin in your gut'. Really interesting stuff. It is said there are certain foods that vast numbers of people consume daily that wreak havoc with your intestinal system. Self-inflicted terrorism on your stomach. I justify office time to complete watching this podcast on the basis that if my physical health improves then so will my mental health, and that can only lead to increased productivity, increased output, and increased money for Management. I am setting my daily agenda here, and this feels right.

Friday, 3.30am
I have been tossing and turning all night. Not in a good way either. I can't sleep. My mind is racing. Thought I might get to sheep number sixteen. No joy. Sheep number fifteen is still impaled on the fence.

I think I am now in a bit of a shit state. Mentally and physically. Maybe it is the middle of the night talking. But I am all edgy and restless. I think I am spending too much time in my own head. Maybe religion is the answer. Never really been one for religion.

I remember a saying from the book of Ivan the Pisshead. Down the local, just before he face planted the bar from a heavy mix of Vodka and Redbull.

"Maxwell, why is it, when you are in your hour of need and all you want to do is to meet god, all you ever get is fucking religion."

Before going looking for God for the answers though I decide to text Noah.

Noah I can't take much more of this. I never thought I would say this. But I need some company. What would you suggest? x

Not expecting an immediate response, I get exactly that.

Eh?

Noah what you doing up at this time.

The question is what the hell are you doing texting me at this time of the morning?

Ok what about a dog? Mans best friend and all that.

Ok. What do I do with a dog?
You feed, water and walk it Max.

I can't walk the dog. We are in lockdown.

Check the rules Max. There is an exception for exercise.

Yes but on your own.

Jesus Maxwell you don't have to stay 2 metres away from animals.

Ok what type?

What about a mix between a bulldog and a Shitsu.

I think for a moment. Then it hits me.

Knob I text back.

4.45am
Finally asleep and dreaming again.

I am in a club about twenty-five years ago. The music is pumping. It's a club in the middle of town. The town I grew up in. Actually, probably the only club in our town. It was called the Crystal Ballroom. The name sounds like something out of the sixties. But that would be deceptive. The Crystal Ballroom was a proper club. All the cool people went there. I am about sixteen, I think. A good age. An irresponsible age. I was on the fringes of being cool.

222

Mandy is there. I have seen her and her mates a few more times in the sweet shop. She has ripped jeans and a white shirt on. Not too much makeup. She didn't need it. I have also had a few drinks. Well, maybe only about two, but enough to make you feel pretty uninhibited at that age. Mandy is giving me the eye. At least I think she is. I get a shot of confidence. I feel like throwing some moves. We are at opposite ends of the dance floor. She is moving like a belly dancer. I am moving my belly. We are getting closer. We will be barn dancing before you know it.

Then the dream becomes a nightmare. I feel a massive blow to my side. Then I am in a headlock. Jesus, this can't be Mandy can it? I mean, this wasn't the nice intimate dancing I was looking for. Then I am being hurled across the dancefloor, I think taking other dancers with me, like some human ten-pin bowling ball. This mother of a man mountain is charging at me all raging bull-like, steam coming out of every orifice. He grabs me by the neck and hurls me out the door. I get up. I look at him. A look that says, 'What the fuck have I ever done to you?'

The man bellows and points at me, really quite treacherously.

And with that the door is slammed in my face. My body and ego are bruised. There is a bloke on my right smoking a cigarette.

"You OK, my friend?" he asks.

"No, not really. That dickhead of a bouncer has just kicked me out for no reason," I say.

"Yeah, looks like you have had a bit of a tough night, kid," the man says. "You need a cigarette?"

"Don't smoke," I say. "Anyway, you could have helped me instead of just standing there."

"Am on me cig break, kid."

"Cig break? Break from what?" I ask.

"Break from being a bouncer," he says.

"A bouncer? You are one of the bouncers here?" I ask.

"That's right," he says.

"So why didn't you help me then?"

"When?" he says.

Is this guy for real? Has he not just seen me thrown like a rag doll out of the place that he is a bouncer of? "Just then. When one of your colleagues kicked me out for minding my own business."

"Just told you. Am on my break."

Jesus Christ. This is the world I am about to grow up in. I force myself to wake up.

50

Start of Eighth Week of Lockdown

Monday, 9.50 am

Today the new 'communications policy' (AKA the policy to ensure no-one is dossing at home) has been activated. There will be several online group meetings, all headed and run by a member of management.

Apparently this is for two official reasons. The first is to test the 'robustness' and 'integrity' of the communications systems, and in particular the new software allowing video conferencing that the firm has chosen to employ. The second is to provide some more information as to working practices during lockdown. For me, I just want to see what other office workers are wearing, and how much weight anyone has either gained or lost in lockdown. To prepare my room I take down the Kylie Minogue and AC/DC pictures. My musical taste is no one else's concern.

I fire up the video conferencing software. There are lots of settings to navigate. Colour, contrast, texture on the aesthetic side. Bass, treble, balance on the audio side. This is fairly complicated. You can mute your microphone completely. Unmute it. I move my laptop camera around. Have they got my good side? How's my hair and makeup? I have a beard. I have never had a beard in my twenty years in the office. Is my beard so bad that it could constitute grounds for unfair dismissal? Is my beard not long enough? There is so much uncertainty here. I need thirty minutes or so on this.

An e-mail pops into my inbox. There has been much more email chatter over the last week. Noticeably so. A whole industry of chancers, conspiracy theorists and opportunistic salespeople have jumped onto the lockdown bandwagon, peddling a whole host of non-essential services, products and self-help guides. My recycling bin has never been so well fed since entering lockdown. This one is entitled 'Spotlight on lockdown – a guide to help your dog cope with lockdown'. Not for me.

10.28am

After twenty minutes or so of tinkering with the settings, checking my lighting, and taking all my posters and pictures down, I restore them all to the factory-recommended settings. It seems the sensible thing to do. No point in showboating here. Hopefully, I can fade into the background in a moment when we are all live and can see each other. Just a beige dull background. Very much like an office should be.

10.29am

I am pacing around a bit. I think it is just hitting me that I have hardly seen or spoken to anyone in weeks.

Just my local shop assistant and that guy from the queue in the supermarket who directed me to a sanitiser station. But now, suddenly I am going to be thrust into some form of online office meeting. How many people will be on it? Do I need to speak? Will the camera get my good side? What about clothes? I have no idea what I should be wearing. In the end I have settled for a polo neck top and tracksuit bottoms. Should I have shaved? Too late for that now.

I click 'join meeting'. Nothing happens immediately.

And then what seems to be an American voice.

"Waiting for the host to start the meeting," she says. "The host knows you are waiting in the lobby."

The lobby? What does that mean? I don't have a lobby. Who does? Why am a waiting in someone's lobby?

Then suddenly there is an influx of pop-ups. Sonia joins the meeting, Karen and Barry join the meeting, suddenly loads more. There is Clare from our office. She must be pissed she can't get to Magaluf. Cameras are being switched on all over the place. The screen is being split 2/4/8/16. People are getting smaller and smaller. More people joining. Some have their video on, some don't. It is all a bit of a free-for-all. It is like some kind of weird video game. All a bit bizarre.

10.35am

No one has said anything yet, but in the last few seconds the screen seems to have stopped splitting. I think that means there isn't any new entrants, so maybe the screen I am looking at now is the final screen.

There must be twenty or so people on my screen. Everyone is looking a bit spaced out. Probably the same look as is on my face currently. The same kind of vacant look that many of the shoppers in the supermarket had. I scan around. Apart from Clare, I don't recognise many of these office workers. But this is unusual. Most are 'dressed down'. This looks like some kind of online art convention, not a team of office workers. People have all kinds of different attire on. Some are in T shirts. There are a few in shirts and ties. And lots of variety in between. It is like everyone is looking at everyone else and trying to see what the majority are wearing. What their background is. What their rooms are like. What their home desks are like. But the only word really to describe the look on the office workers' faces is… well, probably bewilderment. Everyone is looking at everyone else. What are we supposed to do? Say hello to everyone? Do I roll my head around to acknowledge everyone?

If I understood the instructions for the call correctly, it seems that any noise from an office worker and the system thinks that person has something to say, and enlarges that person to fit the whole screen. And that is to be avoided as far as I am concerned. I really don't have enough to say at this stage to be in full screen, not being either Martin Luther King or Gandhi. So the mute function is useful. And the option that turns your video camera off. I hit both buttons.

10.39am
No one has spoken yet. Where is the Management delegate who is supposed to the master of this video

conferencing ceremony? All the faces on the multi-split screen are so small that it could be any one of them. This is like playing the office version of Where's Wally?

Suddenly, "Hello everyone" comes a voice from nowhere. After a couple of seconds' delay, the voice has a full-screen face as the multi-screen suddenly becomes one screen. The face of one of the managers. Damian, I think it is. He has slick jet-black hair, the kind of gel that would get you banned from school chemistry labs, and a particularly red face. He starts talking.

"First and foremost, I hope everyone is OK. And it is really, really great to see you all again. I know this might not be the ideal environment or circumstances, but we have been working hard behind the scenes to make sure we have these kind of video-conferencing facilities in place, so that first and foremost, we can connect with each other again."

I'm actually quite a bit less interested in what he is saying than in what is going on in Damian's house. What I know he won't be telling us is if or when we are going to get essential items for us to do our jobs – stationery, printers, mugs, that kind of thing. But my lockdown shopping trip sorted some of that. The receipt is in my safe. Management will be getting that receipt shortly, whether they like it or not.

No, this is a unique opportunity to check out his home working office. His home. His vibe. It looks like he is in a study. He hasn't had to convert a room to an office. He had an office in the first place. Course he did. Looks to me like he has though strategically placed some contemporary books on the shelf behind him. All sorts of touchy-feely type books. I can make out a few titles. Meditation books, travel books, cookery books. His real reading material, *American Psycho* and *Wall Street*, is probably under his desk.

10.50am

Damian's speech is still going on. It isn't very focused. It certainly isn't holding my attention. Suddenly one of the office workers ups and leaves. Just gets up and leaves his home office. That takes balls. Damian doesn't draw attention to it, but everyone must have clocked it. Maybe he thought he had turned his camera off or something. There is just an empty seat. Maybe he has an Amazon delivery. Several minutes pass before he finally returns. He comes back with a mug in hand, stirring it as he sits back down. He has got up and made a cuppa whilst Damian is in mid-flow. How brazen is that? You couldn't have done that back in the real office. There may be some uses to this home video conferencing.

11.20am

Damian has just closed his presentation. There was a lot of sound bites, but not much in the way of substance. Not much meat on the bones. In particular, I'm still none the wiser as to how to print.

I think there are a few things to take away from this first video home conference call:

1. Damian should set a better example and make sure he is already in his house when he has office workers waiting in his lobby.

2. Damian already had a home office before Covid.
3. Office workers look fucking weird when they are all in dress down and on a video.
4. There are voting buttons on the control bar. You can electronically 'thumbs up' a comment. There is no need to physically put your hand up.
5. If you fart, the software immediately assumes you have something to say and projects you onto the big screen.
6. Masks aren't needed. You can't get Covid over the internet.
7. You can get away with playing hardcore dance music in the background at moments where the meeting is taking a dip, provided you have the mute function on.
8. You should always triple-check that your mute function is on at the moments that you play hardcore dance music in the background.
9. Headstands are great with the camera off. Great for getting good blood flow to the head. That would be good for my hair follicles, which would be good for my confidence, and confidence breeds a good and more productive office worker. So these home online conferencing meetings may be useful for laying the foundations for having a fuller head of hair.

51

End of Eighth Week of Lockdown

Friday, 2pm

There hasn't been much office communication going on this week. Despite the launch of the new software and Damian's speech on Monday, I have had a leisurely week. Still enjoying wearing my lockdown clothes. Still enjoying my commute to the office, down one flight of stairs.

Thoughts turn to fitness. Another unwanted byproduct of this fucking virus. That revolving door of problems keeps spinning. I am putting on about a pound a day. And with no immediate prospect of Boris' hair being brushed or manicured, and redemption day seeming still a world away, that rate won't be sustainable. At this rate, I will be about eighteen stone seven by this time next year. Eighteen stone might work for heavyweight boxers, but not for office workers.

So today, and to avoid obesity, I have spent most of the lunchtime break watching YouTube videos on how to keep fit at home during the lockdown. I save some yoga, some cardio, and some HIIT training videos on my YouTube watchlist. But I think I will crack on with all that tomorrow.

I have started to revisit The Alien Jury to keep myself occupied. I might try to start to write bits here and there. If I can't write anything in a pandemic, when working from home, and with work targets currently suspended, then I won't really be making it as an author any time soon. There is only so long that a book can exist just as a title.

I have heard that people are turning to gaming to get through lockdown. Sales of online console games are going through the roof. Second only to gym equipment. I have never been much of a gamer. But I do enjoy planes. Always have. Maybe I should have been a pilot. Or cabin crew. So I order a flight simulator game pack to keep me occupied for the next fifty weekends. I have deliberately chosen one that has a flight to Australia. In real-time. That will keep me going for most of the weekend. What can you do indoors for twenty-four hours? Fly to Australia on a home computer aviation simulation game.

3.34pm

Oh dear God, I thought it would too good to be true. Nearly nine weeks into lockdown and no e-mails from Daniel. Until now that is. There it is in my inbox. My finger hovers over the mouse. Left click and read or right click and send to junk? I will probably regret this but I left click.

Hello mate!
How you finding things? All OK with you?
Unprecedented times isn't it?

'Unprecedented times'? Daniel doesn't know any words over six letters. He has got that expression from the news.

Anyway, Management doesn't seem to have a Fuc@@@g clue as to what is going on based on the e-mail from the other day, yeah? All a bit tough this, yeah?

Why does he keep using 'yeah' at the end of each sentence?

Are you able to get anything done? Don't miss the traffic in the morning. Anyway, e-mail me. Would be good to keep connected until we are back in.
Thought I would let you know I have some masks with holes in them so you can keep them on when you are eating. Let me know if you need a batch. See you on the other side!

I have no further thoughts on this. But I do have a slightly strange and unanticipated response. I am actually pleased to have received an e-mail. Even from Daniel.

52

Ninth Week of Lockdown

Thursday – 2am

I see an object ahead of me, slightly blurry, as if I am wearing the wrong glasses. I am staring at the object, trying desperately to make it out. My mouth is open, as it always is when I am concentrating. But steadily and slowly the object starts to focus. It looks a little like a man. A small man. But still a man. But I can't make out a face. The man seems to be floating, hovering in the air like some sort of wizard. It is coming closer. Please don't let this be Jim from Accounts again. Not again.

As it gets closer I start to make it out. Jesus, it doesn't seem to have a face. It is a... suit, shirt and tie, alone, just floating in the air. Like on a mannequin that doesn't exist. There is nobody in it. Just a faceless, lifeless blacked-out mannequin, but in a suit and tie. It is just billowing on the breeze, the shirt is un-ironed, the tie I think has what looks like food stains on it. Purple food stains. Suddenly a massive hand shoots into view, getting bigger and bigger and opening up as it is getting closer and closer to the airborne suit and tie combo. And then the massive hand open's up completely and envelopes the faceless suit and tie. There is just blackness for a split second and then suddenly, in an explosion of fire and light, the massive hand takes its prey to the heavens, getting smaller and smaller as it ascends. I can't quite make it out anymore. Maybe that is it. Maybe that is the end of this dream.

Moments pass. And then suddenly the object gets bigger again. What was a small dot is expanding. It is coming back towards Earth, getting bigger and bigger, and building up a head of steam. Closer and closer and closer until bang! It drives the suit and tie straight into the ground, the ground trembling like a factor thirty earthquake until eventually there is quiet.

Wake up, Maxwell, you bastard; wake up, you big useless bastard. I can't be a spectator to my office suit and tie's destruction. This is even worse than the freight train dream.

"Nooo, take me instead!" I howl into the darkness of the crater. "Leave my office clothes alone. It's me that you want. Me, me, ME…"

I bolt up on my bed. There is sweat all over my bedclothes. At least, I assume it is sweat. No, it is just sweat. Thank God for that at least. My lockdown dreams are getting worse. Sweat is always a sign of really bad dreams.

I need to speak to someone about these dreams. But the NHS isn't even removing ear wax at the moment, let alone listening to my dreams of being hit by freight trains and big hands and suits. Lennox, like the milkman, is still AWOL. Wendy has enough on her plate. This is about me now. And my own resilience. If I have any.

3am

Still can't sleep after the horrific dream a while back with the faceless suit and tie. I get the vacuum cleaner out, lay it on its back, and turn it on. I sometimes turn to the vacuum cleaner as a last resort. High pitched white noise to get me to sleep. I never told Lennox that I occasionally used the vacuum cleaner. Despite his duty of confidentiality, he always had the potential power to section me.

8am

Wake up to the sound of the vacuum cleaner. It isn't the normal sound though. It is a really horrible high-pitched wailing. I think the fuse might have gone or something. At least I got some sleep though.

12 noon

This is driving me mad. Since being at home, my laptop has been operating at a shit speed. Just one full stop remaining in this document and then bang, the cursor stops working. Frozen screen. Currently I am experiencing the blue circle of death. Just whirring around. I am not some doormat of an office worker to some jumped-up piece of computer coding. Someone needs to be held accountable for this. Who is my internet provider? They are going to get some.

I dial the customer number.

12.14pm

On hold to the internet provider.

12.19pm

Just got through the hold music. Into the number options now.

12.25pm

Just got through the number options. Option one is the one that I wanted. How they needed ten minutes to direct me to option one, only they know. Still, I must be through to a human shortly.

"Hello," comes a somewhat downbeat voice.

"I am currently home working at the moment, and I seem to have a very patchy connection to the internet. I often get frozen screens, blue circles, things like that."

"What kind of time are you getting most of this?" the downbeat internet bloke says.

"Usually between about ten and two it is at its worst."

"Yeah, makes sense," the man says, still not full of beans.

"Excuse me?" I say.

"So you will do. Get downtime around that time I mean. The whole country is logging on these days about that time, you know. The system isn't designed for that kind of abuse all at the same time. So you are gonna get a bit of interference. Not much we can do at the moment about that. It should settle down in time."

Settle down in time? I don't have piles.

"So there is nothing you can do about it then?"

"Not unless I can cut the internet usage to your neck of the woods by about fifty percent. And that would mean knocking on a lot of houses," the man laughs sarcastically. He clearly enjoys his own jokes.

"OK, no worries then," I say, upping the sarcasm level.

"Just before you go, can you just take part in a quick survey? That will cover stuff like how easy it is to get through to us, the quality of the service and the likelihood of recommending us to others based on past use."

I hang up.

53

Tenth Week of Lockdown

Monday, 6.30am

My phone is buzzing. Who the hell is that at this time of day? Can't be work. Might be Wendy. No. It is a text from an unknown number.

Maxwell. Open your curtains!

Eh? This must be a wind-up. Its 6.30 on a Monday morning and it is still – at least, the last time I looked – yes, it is still a lockdown situation. I open my curtains, squinting through the darkness to work out what is going on. It is all dark. Apart from a spotlight. A small spotlight. I can't really make it out. Suddenly a brighter light goes on. It is a man on a bike. Wearing Lycra. You are kidding me. Can it be? Yes, it seems like it is. This time I don't think I am dreaming. It can only be Tony. It *is* Tony. Tony the office cyclist. He is frantically waving at me. He also seems to have a pandemic mask on. Bright green also. I am not sure he is at high risk of getting Covid on a bike, outside and at 6.30 in the morning. But at least he has made the effort.

I raise a hand back in semi acknowledgment. I am still half asleep. Not much more I can do, really. I can't ask him in. That would be breaking the law. I think about opening the window and shouting to him. But he wouldn't hear me over his Lycra. After a moment or two of waving at each other, he disappears off into the darkness.

How that man has the energy I will never know. And in a lockdown. 6.30am in the morning in the middle of a pandemic. It doesn't look like there was an ounce of fat on him either. His wave is still the same. It wasn't some beaten, submissive wave. It was joyful, defiant. I probably shouldn't have expected anything less. That wave spoke volumes. Maybe that is the way forward for me? Buy some bright Lycra, get a bike and give a monumental two fingers up to Covid. Quite inspirational really.

Nice gesture that, my friend. I go back to bed.

4pm

The last thing on my short list for homeworking for today is to link up my PC to the printer I bought a few weeks ago from the supermarket. It still isn't operational. The technical term for this is tethering. This is not going well. Ten minutes in and I'm still nowhere with the tethering. I can now forget tethering my PC to my new printer. The only tether going on today is the one that I am at the end of. I can't work this printer. I might as well have been trying to tether my laptop to a printer in Scotland. In fact, I probably have. Some poor Scot is probably running out of paper just about now. I bring my working day to an end.

6.30pm

I can't quite believe I am doing this. But for some reason I have agreed to an online virtual date from the dating website that Noah sent me. I got a date request a week ago. I have been hovering all week between accepting and rejecting it. In the end I accepted it. I don't know why. There are some things in life you can't logic. This would be one of them. Apparently the person I am to meet is over a 70% match.

So I am currently sat in the kitchen with my laptop. I have spent a bit of time positioning my laptop, got the lighting in the kitchen right, and tweaked the background a bit. I have chosen to wear a light grey jumper (not polo neck, obviously) and shorts. The shorts are purely for comfort, not for fashion. I wouldn't be wearing shorts on a real date, pre-pandemic.

I'm not sure if I should put aftershave on. I decide against doing so. She won't be able to smell it. But maybe I will feel like I am getting more into the spirit of this.

I also have a small beer with me. I have chosen not to be drunk though. That wouldn't be an encouraging start. Especially because on my questionnaire I had said I was in the 3-7 unit category of alcohol consumption a week. Suddenly a face pops up on the screen. There is a slight pause. She is looking at me and I am looking at her. It is all a bit panicky from both of us. It seems clear neither of us are seasoned at this.

She has short black hair, a forehead, definitely two eyes and I am sure she also has a nose. All a good start.

She seems quite nice on a first look. I suddenly feel quite self-conscious.

I am not very focused, I can feel it. There are a few thoughts clouding my mind:

1. Why am I doing this?
2. Why is this lady doing this?
3. How long is this date for?
4. I should have prepped for this. I really don't know what to say.

"Hiya," she suddenly says after a few seconds' pause from both of us. "I'm Sam."

"Hi Sam. I am Maxwell."

"Hi Maxwell. Nice to virtually meet you."

An uncomfortable pause.

"So, is Sam short for Samantha?" I ask.

Jesus Christ. Did I really just say that out loud?

Moron.

She laughs. Slightly I think. Not really a genuine laugh. The kind of laugh that says 'I should laugh' rather than 'I want to laugh'.

"Yes it is. So what brings you to this website then?" she asks.

"Erm, well…" I am already floundering. Good question. What am I doing on this website?

"Well, it was actually a friend of mine who works in my local coffee house. He suggested I should try it."

"Well, I am glad he did. And how long have you been on the site? Have you mixed much yet?"

"No actually, you are my first. I don't mean my first in that sense. I mean the first person I have spoken to."

What am I saying? You bastard, Noah, for making me do this.

She laughs again. I didn't mean that to be funny so this isn't doing much for my confidence.

"So apparently we are compatible," Sam carries on. "Not sure how a computer works that out, but there you go."

"Yes, I thought that was a bit odd myself. That questionnaire took ages."

Good, measured reply, Maxwell, I think. Maybe I am getting into my stride now. Need to make sure I don't swear. Not on the first date. I take a sip of my beer to make me look a bit cool. For some reason my little finger is pointing outwards.

Samantha hasn't got a drink on her table as far as I can see. She has really nice blinds, though, in the windows behind her. Really well fitted. Nice flower arrangement on the shelf. I reckon she has done this before. I myself am an online virgin.

"So what are you wearing?" I suddenly ask.

Where did that come from? I can see what she is wearing up top. So the only reason I just asked that, she must be thinking, is because I am a pervert. Which I am not. But she won't know that.

There is a pause. She looks a bit worried, then lets out a massive laugh.

"How about you stand up, Maxwell? I will show you mine if you show me yours."

I am on the wrong website. Are we entering erotica here?

I can't stand up though. I have shorts on and brown socks. I hadn't prepared for either erotica or standing up.

I think I have two options. Either go with it and risk looking like a moron or a pervert or both or act like my internet connection is unstable. I choose to go for the latter. I don't think I can do this. I switch the laptop off.

6.52pm

It has been two minutes since I ended the call with Samantha, abruptly and without notice.

I am not proud of myself. I feel bad. But I couldn't show her my shorts. And I am not ready to either get into erotica or deeply emotional conversations. I realise I am completely not ready for this online flirting. Noah is wrong.

Before coming off this website for the rest of my life, I have a rummage around. I am currently browsing some of the other male members on this dating app. God, there are hundreds of people on this thing. The whole world has gone online. *No you are joking.* I take a sharp intake of breath, and forget for a moment to exhale. The reason: Jim from Accounts is on here. I'd know that face anywhere. He is not in a suit and tie. But it is definitely Jim from Accounts. What is he doing on here? How could he want a companion? He needs to be on a specialist website, not on this surely? I immediately delete my profile. I can't take the risk. I need a drink.

9pm

Still traumatised. I don't think I will be sleeping anytime soon tonight. I try to read a bit. I bought a book a little while ago, before we entered lockdown actually. It was suggested to me by Lennox. I haven't opened it yet. I think I will tonight. This book is entitled, *You might not be able to change the world, but you can change the world in you.*

The back page suggests that the main thrust of the book is that I need to have regard for my emotional, physical and mental wellbeing. Get those building blocks in place and I will be back on track. Exercise the mind and body. I feel like it might be time to put this into action.

It has quite a few reviews. Most are positive. They seem to be along the lines of 'I used to be a bit of an idiot, but having read this book my friends have commented that I have become a little less of an idiot'.

After hanging up on Samantha I may need to take a good, long, hard look at myself. Maybe this book is a first step.

54

Still Tenth Week of Lockdown

Tuesday, 6am

Energised from my self-help bedtime reading the night before, I wake up. Waking up is always a good start. Not to be granted these days. A pre-requisite to the day, really. I wake up really early. Bollocks to the late morning. Time for a bit of a fight back. Small victories in the bigger war.

Physically though, I look like shit. Covid has done a number on me, even though I don't think I have actually had the virus yet. Lockdown has given me resting bastard face. I might have to consider botox. I need to get some pride back. I am a vision of junk food at the moment. Cut me open and you would find undigested kebabs and fast food. Very little fruit and veg. My selection of pyjamas and slinky dressing gowns is masking the increasing fatty tissue around the waist and nipple areas. I need to assume there will be a time in the next ten years when Boris has stabilised his haircut, and we will be back to the office.

A minute later I am out of bed, doing some stretching. I am going to kick this new locked down fitness regime off. I don't even feel the need to put any clothes on for this. Some bits are hanging out. But I am not self-conscious. I am stretching like there is no tomorrow.

6.30am

As dawn is breaking I am in the middle of my home workout. Not the spit and sawdust gym-type workout. Not heavy weights and spotting. This involves a bit of cardio, some light resistance and a lot of sedentary poses, which the lockdown instructor I have found on YouTube seems to suggest are working both mind and body. I am slightly less convinced on these elongated and still poses, though. Just stretch in one direction and then hold it for about twenty minutes. That is generally what I do in bed. But there must be something to this. The whole world seems to be on it. And Gwyneth Paltrow and Chris Martin, obviously.

8.50am

I am at my desk, giving myself ten minutes to log on. The body has had a workout. Now for the mind. Time to get stuck into some work.

Come on, Maxwell, pull your finger out.

I peruse my calendar for the day. I have my coffee. I have ironed a shirt. I tried to cut at the ends of my beard with some blunt scissors. I feel a bout of invigoration. Maybe we need a bit of a co-ordinated fight back. Everyone has been running scared of Covid. All our brains have been scrambled from the Covid punch to the temple. But maybe we should start to get off the canvass. Beat the count. Science and medicine will solve this problem. Why wouldn't they? And I think I need to do my bit also. If everyone does their bit, does their job, then we will get there. Humanity will get there. I need to mark this moment. I need to get my Winston Churchill outfit on, shave a bald patch into the back of my head, put on a fatsuit, and smoke a massive cigar. And then go into the street with a megaphone. Get the steel drums involved. Maybe a tambourine or a trombone. Motivate the street. Word will get round.

So this is rapidly becoming a celebratory day. A progressive day. I am staring in the mirror of my bathroom. I think of the song "The Man in the Mirror" by Michael Jackson. I don't believe that that song is about vanity, or dying your hair, or advanced plastic surgery. No I don't. I think it is about what is inside, not on the outside. Like my new self-help book says, I can't change the world, but I can change the world in me. And what of the office? The *people are* the office. My colleagues, my co-workers. The heart and soul. The people. All of them. Jim from Accounts. Tony, Clive, Clare. Even Daniel, on his less annoying days. There is still some good in him, I know it. My colleagues are relying on me, and I am relying on them. We all need to do our bit to keep the commercial wheels turning. Get the world back in the game. Humanity has been down before, but rarely defeated. I can't rely on the government, Boris or the IT department to tell me what to do. I rely on me. If everyone relies on themselves then we will have this thing beat. And anything else that feeling like fucking with our collective human spirit and resilience in the future. It is time for me to grab the bull by the horns and ride it. Love is bigger than anything in its way.

So that is it all in a nutshell. The fight back starts right here, and right now. For the rest of today, I will be putting together a daily routine. If I can't go to the gym, the gym will come to me. No radio on in the day. We aren't allowed it at work, why should I be allowed it in my office? No feet up on the desk. No slouching.

Return the lumbar to a vertical position. I will even allocate some time to health and safety.

And with all that structure back, I am surely back on the path to productivity. Let's pull some hope from the jaws of defeat.

I feel like this day needs a name. Yes, this feels like a rebirth. A resetting of the clock. Resetting my mind, body, and everything in between. I will call this day 'the office worker rising like a fucking phoenix from the flames day'. Actually that's a bit wordy. "Redemption day." Yes, that will do.

Part 3

55

The Next Few Weeks of Lockdown After Redemption Day

The malaise

In the end the initial euphoria of redemption day proved to be short-lived. Things started to take a turn for the worse after that. The monotony of locked down living in the last few weeks has proved relentless, an unstoppable train of bleakness ploughing through any semblance of positivity. News on the virus hasn't been good. Talk of variants, whatever the fuck that means. Omnicron. Delta. They all sound like bad bond villains to me. Boris's hair is becoming unmanageable and his instructions on how to socialize have become as confusing as his hair. There is something called the rule of six. To do with how households can now interact. Great idea I am sure. All based on sound medical advice from the Chief Medical officer. But I don't think any fucker in the whole of the United Kingdom knows what it means. It will be the Magnificent Seven next. Maybe then the Hateful Eight. Anyway not sure I need to worry about the rule of six, given that I might be struggling to find five people who currently want to socially interact with me.

Hours, days, weeks merged into one. Fitness regimes slipped. Alcohol intake has increased. I bought more fish-themed dressing gowns online. I haven't been able to get past chapter one of any of my self help books. I have been travelling more long-haul routes on my flight simulator game. I have now ordered a full captains uniform. It hasn't arrived yet. None of this could be viewed as any kind of a return to normalcy. And my work productivity? In the gutter.

It is a measure of how bad the last few weeks have gotten that a positive day has been finding a pair of socks that didn't have holes in them. The drinks cabinet has been shut for a couple of weeks, then in a fit of rage and weakness a couple of weeks ago I ripped the drinks cabinet's hinges off in a frenzied pursuit of whiskey induced escapism. I have looked into hiring a welder for the drinks cabinet.

My lockdown working hours have been reducing still further. All my life as an office worker has been about routine. Structure. Routine. A bit more structure. I didn't think about it. All of that suddenly replaced with freedom, flexibility, autonomy. I am in charge of my daily routine. All the stuff that I thought I craved. But as the days and weeks have passed, this has all started to feel wrong. You only appreciate stuff when it isn't there anymore. I never thought that could apply to the office or a daily office routine. I thought work was the boring bit. The monotonous bit. Maybe I was wrong.

56

Sixteenth Week of Lockdown

Monday, 3am
Beach scene

The sun is shining. There are blue skies everywhere. Temperatures are around twenty degrees Celsius. Pleasant. Not hot enough to burn but hot enough to be in light, casual clothes. This seems like spring, maybe even summer. There's not a cloud in the sky. Even those cumulonimbus clouds that geography teachers used to go on about, even they aren't in the sky. This scene is idyllic. I am sitting here basking in the sun on one of those hammocks you see on package holidays to the Seychelles. I am holding a beer in one hand, my phone in the other. There are several people in this scene. Mostly people from the office. To my left is Jim from Accounts. He is smiling from ear to ear. He has a light beige suit and beige tie on. He is on a swing. His smile would melt the hardest of hearts. This smile is a million miles away from the ironic, twisted smile on the front of the freight train from an earlier nightmare. This is a smile that says... well, it says 'joy'.

The hardest of human emotions to show. Pure joy. He is mouthing something each time he hits the top of the swing. He is counting his swings. I think he is on about one hundred and sixty-seven.

I look to my right. There they are, running around and jumping in the hay fields: Howard and Tim from the print room. They are holding hands, a right couple of lovebirds. They have white loose-fitting suits on. Tim has a tie on, obviously. They both have flowers in their hair. One word comes to mind watching them both. Liberation – from the print room.

In the distance, I hear Daniel. He is singing. I think it sounds like something from the *Sound of Music*. Quite uplifting.

There is a road in the middle. A beautifully laid, totally even road. No potholes. The kind of road that probably doesn't exist in real life. The best road you could ever wish for. There is a speck in the distance. A bright yellow speck. Bright yellow Lycra on metal. It is Tony moving effortlessly on his bike. It looks like he is in the right gear. As he passes me he is waving again. Obviously. No pandemic mask on this time.

I am in my best office suit. It is white with some gold lamé edging. It has my initials carved into the interior. It is the mother of all suits. I feel something tight around my neck. I think I may have a tie on.

4.30am

I bolt up in bed so hard that I think my head momentarily meets my shaft.

My head is starting to clear. I am still breathing

heavily. Come on, calm down, Maxwell, you are awake now. None of that is real. It was all created in the dark recesses of your tired, lockdown-addled brain. But what was that one all about? That is probably the most disturbing lockdown dream of all.

I need some time to figure this out.

I go downstairs in my dressing gown to the kitchen. The kitchen has become my new thinking area. My zone of contemplation. And the chair in the kitchen, an old, decrepit, quite uncomfortable hardbacked chair, has become my new throne of contemplation. I sit on my new throne of contemplation and try to work it out. What is going on with me? What is going on with my dreams?

I have had a series of unexplainable and really quite frightening dreams. And then, just a few moments ago, I have been dreaming about Jim from Accounts in a beige suit and on a swing? I have no idea where it was. But it can't be Magaluf otherwise Clare would have been there.

I can't figure this out. This is way bigger than me. And I certainly can't ask anyone. I am just sitting here. Motionless. Trying to make sense of it all. Trying to make sense of the world, the pandemic, me, my dreams. I can't crack that quickly. After two years, Lennox still hasn't given me a good reason as to why sheep number fifteen keeps being impaled on the fence.

I think the past three months is starting to catch up with me. I think I may also be dribbling just a little bit from the side of my mouth…

57

Moment of Surrender

6.50 am – later the same day

I am still sitting there. Same position. Rigor mortis will be setting in soon. I can't remember the last time I blinked. Dawn is just starting to break.

Suddenly I feel waves of emotions come over me. Just floods of emotions. Just all suddenly welling up. I can't take this anymore, holed up at home, on my own, living in my head. Eating cheese and beetroot sandwiches. Having no one to turn to when I cut through my hedge cutters. I think I might have some tears in my eyes. These are not tears of joy.

This may be the moment of realisation. The moment of surrender. I need my office back. I need my colleagues back. I need structure back. Routine back. The commute back.

I need the flash of colour that is Tony the cyclist. I need the daily mental workout of trying to avoid Jim from Accounts. I want to see if the man in the coffee house that reminds me of a llama will ever order something different. I want Charlie to say good morning to me. I want to see Tim take over from Howard one day in the post room.

I want the challenge of Felix Doberman trying to

get one over on me. I want my senses violated by the office slurper. Yes, I do. I really do. I want to feel the adrenaline rush of possibly using someone else's baby mug and getting abused in public for it. And yes, I may even need my old nemesis, my office arch-enemy, Daniel. This is a moment of surrender for me.

I fall to my knees on the kitchen floor. When will this lockdown end? When?... WHEN?...

58

A Few Weeks Later

Sunday, 8pm
The evening before the morning after
This evening is no ordinary Sunday evening. We were, a few weeks ago, given the potential green light by Boris for a tentative return to the office. Even though his hair has remained largely unkempt through the whole process. In the end Boris's hair was not a barometer of the status of the pandemic. The reason for the return has been mainly the new vaccine programme. Medicine on the fightback. Fasttrack jab. A rapid rollout programme.

So today, this Sunday evening is a very, very different Sunday evening. This is the day before the big return. *The return to the office.* A momentous day. A day many of us genuinely thought would never come.

Office life is to look very different though. There will be loads of safety protocols in place. Number one is masks. Masks will be the new norm. I have less issue with that. I am starting to get used to masks. I have ten packs of ten. All brown. Sanitiser stations will be everywhere in the office. I hope they are better than the sanitiser stations in my local shop, which, to be honest, never have any sanitiser in them – so all you are doing is touching something that everyone else has touched but without the ability to clean your hands just after as it has no soap in it. So they're basically a spreader of disease. Printers will be out of action as major potential spreaders of viruses. Mugs and kitchens, we are told, will be off-limits. Further spreaders of disease. I didn't realise how many things in an office can spread a virus. How were we not all off with E-coli before the pandemic?

We won't be back full-time though. Not yet. There is to be some form of new 'hybrid' working arrangement. Three days a week in the office, two days at home. Something like that. Or maybe it is two days in the office, three days at home. It is all a bit unclear.

Tonight feels like starting again. Starting in the office for the first time. As a young office worker. That same mix of nerves and excitement. Ready to do what it takes in the office. Prepared to climb the greasy office pole. That's how I feel now. I will take my time this Sunday evening, making sure Monday goes as smoothly as possible. Before the pandemic I used to always get my shit together the evening before. Used to cut down my morning routine time and stress. No reason to change that side of things in the post pandemic world.

So that means, in terms of my clothes, that I make sure that the following occurs:

1. My suit is ironed and pressed.
2. My suit and tie are colour coordinated.

3. My socks are matching.
4. My underpants are freshly laundered and occasionally ironed.
5. The whole outfit is then laid out in the order that I need to dress. Laid out on the floor, socks on the far left, tie being far right. Everything else in between.

Then comes the shoes. Office shoes are one of the most important parts of the uniform. Nothing says more about the office worker than the state of his shoes. I started my office career with the shiniest shoes. Part of my evening routine was scrubbing them until I could see my face in them. But over the years, like so many initial office routines, standards slipped. Just so long as your office trousers don't ride up on the boot tops at the back. Looking like John Wayne is not the right look in any office. Tonight, I shine my shoes for a good ten minutes.

I look in the mirror. I look like Tom Hanks from *Castaway*. Hair all over the place. Not just on my head. And the beard. Jesus, how am I going to get through this bastard. I have thirteen individuals razors. This will take a while…

59

The Return of the Max

Monday, 7.15am
First day back in the office
Prior to lockdown I would have just been getting up around this time for a Monday in the office.

But I have been up for a good hour already. I am already in my office suit and tie, pack of masks at the ready, and on my throne of contemplation, sat in the kitchen with a cup of water and really looking forward to getting back to civilisation. I am really quite emotional. I feel a slight tear. Or is that my dry eye condition flaring again?

It feels like the first day at school. I have the same feeling as I did when I was holding a satchel, in short trousers, and walking into school with my mum. Hopefully I don't wet myself this time though.

After all these months in isolation have I forgotten how to talk to people? How to construct a sentence? What will lockdown have done to Daniel's fragile mental state? Concern about getting too close to people with a slight cough. Concern about wearing my mask the wrong way round.

8.14am

I am walking through town on my way to work after the train. The train was on time this morning. Spot on time. To the second, nearly. I suppose the train company has had a good period in lockdown to get their house in order. It will be back to being late tomorrow probably. As I walk the old usual walk to the office, reality hits. This isn't like I remembered it. Lots of shop fronts are boarded up. Many others have gone. Looks like the economic apocalypse has just hit my town centre. Maybe I shouldn't have expected anything else. Machines don't make all this stuff work. People do. And people have been hit pretty fucking badly in the last couple of years.

There are a few people around but the atmosphere is subdued. I stand looking at one boarded-up shop. There is graffiti all over it. I don't think I had ever looked at graffiti before. Not properly. I just assumed that it was some aggrieved youth with the world on his shoulders. But maybe this is someone's idea of expression. They probably shouldn't do it on someone else's property though.

8.19am

Steadily walking the route to the office. There is a calmness to my steps; I'm less frantic than when I used to walk to the office before the pandemic. There is less concern about being late. I pass another boarded-up shop. I am sure that used to be a hairdresser's. On the front is a sign saying 'Axe throwing – coming soon'.

Fucking hell. This is a new world.

8.22am

I don't mind admitting it. I am really quite excited. I am nearly at the coffee house.

I turn the corner. Previously, and pre-pandemic, that would have been away from the hustle and bustle. Away from the hustle and bustle and noise of morning people going about their business, and to the relative calm and tranquility of the backstreet to the coffee house. But the distinction isn't really there today. The effect is not as it once was. Today I am looking for more noise, not less.

There are a couple of people on the street. In suits. Like me they look like it is their first day back in the office. There is a homeless person in one of the doorways. As I pass him he smiles.

"Any change mate." he says.

"Ok my friend?" I say. I take out £2 and hand it to him.

"God bless you" he says.

"So… how have you been" I ask tentatively.

"Eh?"

"You know… what with Covid and lockdown and all that."

"Fuck all changed for me pal. People have been keeping their distance from me for years!"

Blimey. I feel like the one sitting down after that. I give him a half smile.

"So could I ask you something?" I say.

"Course matey. Aint got nowhere to be. I have all the time in the world."

"So how do you, you know..err."

"Fucking spit it out mate" he says "I haven't got all day" he laughs.

"So how do you, get through the loneliness, not having anyone to talk to... you know the boredom of it all."

"Good question mate, glad you finally got there. So that would be by dreaming."

"Dreaming?"

The homeless man points to his head.

"Yeah, dreaming pal. I can close my eyes at any point in the day, and go off to whatever place I want to in my mind."

And I thought dreams were a bad thing.

"Dream out loud brother, that's what I say. Now fack off and let me get on with my day."

8.45am

The coffee house is in sight. I doesn't look like it is boarded up. Thank fuck for that. I open the door. The familiar sound of that little, quaint, apologetic bell is music to my ears. That bell is still working. Might have a bit of rust on it. Possibly e-coli as I doubt Noah would have ever cleaned it. But it is still doing the job it was designed for. All through lockdown and beyond. It doesn't need batteries or electricity. Just needs someone to go in the shop for it to kick in to life. In a world of technology, that little bell is still going.

There is a bit of a pause. There is no one else in here. "Maxwell, my friend!" comes a voice from out back. "Noah ! As I live and breathe, you are alive!"

"Course I am, Maxwell. Someone got to keep the population fed and watered."

He comes over from behind the counter, arms aloft in hug formation. I pause and then he pauses. We look at each other. What is the rule? Are we breaking the law by hugging? Are we members of each other's household? I think we are both thinking the same thing. Fuck it, we are going to have a hug.

We hug for about thirty-five seconds. Neither of us wants to give up first.

"Er, Noah," I say, still in mid clinch.

"Yes Max?"

"This is all really great and that but I think you might have your hand fully on my ass now."

"Oh yes, you are right, Max. Let's save that for another day."

"Anyway, I thought you would have been saving your hugs for the well-dressed purple-haired lady. You know the one you keep trying it on with, you know, the one out of your league."

Noah laughs.

"So yeah, seen her quite a bit, Maxwell, lately. We reopened about a week ago and she has been in. There haven't been many other regulars, obviously. Hopefully that will start to pick up now. Think she works around here though, that lady. I think she does something like you. You know, a pen-pusher and all that."

"Yeah, you can't fool me. You didn't even know I was here last time I was in when she was here. I even nearly cracked my head on your doorstep, which you won't recall as you were at that moment gazing into her eyes. So any developments with her then?"

"Never mind about my love life, Maxwell. What about yours, my friend? You get that link I sent you? How many virtual dates did you have in lockdown?"

"One, Noah. And it will stay at one. It was a fucking disaster. It was so bad I had to turn the power off. It traumatised me and probably traumatised the lady I was having the date with. I blame you entirely for that."

"If you tell me you don't want to meet someone else then tell me that. But until you do, I will keep sending through links. You can't stop me. This was a free country last time I looked. You might be able to block me on text or WhatsApp but you can't block an e-mail. I am going to keep working on you Maxwell."

"So speaking of Covid, what's your take on it all?" I say.

"There you go, not even a subtle change of subject, Max. To be continued, my friend, to be continued."

"Yeah, whatever Noah. Anyway, Covid. Lockdown. The pandemic. What's your take on it?"

"Maxwell, I have been anticipating this question from you for weeks. I had this whole speech ready. You know, went through all the emotions that everyone else did when Covid hit. Mainly anger. I know you were probably anticipating a whole speech. But you know what, Max?"

"What, Noah?"

"In the end I thought no, I am not going to talk about Covid. Covid doesn't deserve it. I don't want to give that bastard the satisfaction of having any more air time, my friend."

"OK mate. I see what you are saying. That was a bit of a speech though, if I am honest."

"Really? Remind me never to ask you to be my best man if you think that was a speech."

"But I probably agree with you Noah. Nothing much more to say on the subject. Lets move on. And from now on, if either of us uses the term 'Covid', the other should punch that person in the face. Deal?"

"Yeah, agreed Max. Agreed."

"So back to the important stuff. Give me my usual then, my friend."

"Maxwell – it has been months since I served you. How am I supposed to remember what your usual is?"

"Give me a minute. I will remember it."

"Well, whilst you are thinking, Maxwell, I might as well give you my thought for the day. I have been working on this for the last eighteen months."

"So this better be good then."

"You gotta keep dancing, even when the lights go out."

Did Noah see me gyrating that morning in lockdown in front of my suit and tie?

60

Where's Charlie?

8.40am

After about fifteen minutes of further headscratching between Noah and I as to what my usual drink is after all this time apart, I am holding a basic latte to go. I have a few minutes so take a bit of a detour to where Lennox's counselling suite is. It isn't too far away and I haven't heard anything of him over Lockdown. I have a bad feeling about this.

8.45am

Arriving at Lennox's place. It isn't boarded up but there are no lights on, no sign of life and just a handwritten note on the door saying 'Closed until further notice'. There are a load of old food wrappers and cans on the floor. Some homeless person has been using his entrance to sleep.

8.59am

There she is again. The office. The same massive glass building. It all still looks the same. I count the floors just to make sure they are all still there. This is a very odd feeling. I take a moment again, just to take it in.

The reception seems to be the same. Obviously there are sanitiser stations everywhere. I try the one on the outside of the main doors. It seems to be operational. I get a bit of soap on my suit. The first of many I should imagine. On the floor of reception there are also yellow signs everywhere. This is a system everyone is now pretty familiar with. Same as in all the supermarkets during lockdown. One way, social distancing, pedestrian calming measures. Whatever you want to call it.

Where's Charlie though? He isn't on reception. On reception is someone I haven't seen before. All masked up obviously.

"Good morning," the chap says. "Good to have you back."

"Yes, good to be back." I say.

Charlie must not be back yet then. Odd to not see him in reception though. I can count on one hand the number of times over the years that Charlie hasn't been on the door. Feels odd. Not quite right.

One of the lifts is out. There's yellow crosses over it. Some things don't change…

In the one, post pandemic operational lift, there is a 'one in' policy. It used to be that the lift couldn't take more than, about 30 stones. I never knew how to adhere to that. It would have meant talking to my fellow liftee's to ask them their weight. To check we weren't exceeding the permitted maximum. But now this is just one person. Don't matter how much you weigh. Actually that is more cilivised.

Stepping into the lift and there is a yellow circle right in the middle, on the floor. Right smack bang in

271

the middle of the lift. It has foot signs on it suggesting (if not instructing you), to face the back of the lift. That is probably a step too far. If there is only one person allowed in the lift, why the fuck do you need to, not only stand in the middle of the lift, but also face towards the back of the lift? Now is not the time to question though. I do as instructed, and stand on the yellow sign facing the back of the lift.

9.01am
Back at my desk. Wow. Very strange feeling.

Daniel arrives. Even stranger. Not that Daniel is here, but that my irritation level is, well, at a very low level. Almost non-existent. And I haven't spoken to Lennox for months.

"Yes, Maxwell!" Daniel greets me as I take my seat. I look at him. I think of all the daft things he has said over the years. I think of all the daft things he is still going to say. And then I smile. That's OK. That's all actually OK. I do something next that I didn't think I would ever do.

I raise my hand for a high five with Daniel. He obliges. "Hey Daniel. So where's Charlie?"

"You haven't heard? Charlie passed away, Maxwell. Covid-related, so I am told. Poor bugger."

I sink back in my seat. Punched in the face with a massive dose of reality. I realise this is just about the first time I have known anyone die from this thing. It had all felt a bit unreal up to know. Just stuff on social media and the news. But this makes it real. I sit back. Not Charlie. Everyone in the building knew Charlie.

The gatekeeper to the office. He was devoted to the office. He cared about the people in this building. You couldn't have done his job if you didn't. He was a man who had his heart firmly in the right place. This will hit anyone who has been in this place more than 5 minutes pretty hard I reckon. Collective grief. This has put a dampener on the day.

5.10pm
Leaving the office. It had started promisingly, but the Charlie news has been a blow. Still, life has to go on, and office life did at least start back up today.

We had a bit more clarity on the hybrid policy. Basically you can work from the office all the time, but if you want to, and if you are set up to work from home, then you can work from home two days a week. I think I have had enough of working from home. I think I will be in the office more often than not from now on.

61

Tuesday Afternoon

There is a big room on the top floor where networking events were held pre-Covid. And today, after about 2 years out the office completely, and now several weeks back in the office, a networking event is about to be held. Known as the drinks room, this room hosted internal meetings, seminars, breakfast briefings, mass redundancy consultations. This room has also over the years occasionally housed the office Christmas party. On that basis alone this room would have some stories to tell. It would have seen a fair number of office worker indiscretions over the years. New starters having too much to drink and throwing up all over the coat rack, office romances, office break ups, office affairs, even possibly some office erotica moments. That kind of stuff. Everyone knows this is the room where, if there is any stuff to go off, it goes off here.

I am at the name badge table just outside the room. Everyone has name badges at these kinds of events. These badges are degrading. They have your name and your company on them. Fully grown adults should not in any circumstances have to wear name badges. That is for toddlers at parties, or prisoners. There are less name badges than before Covid. No matter. This is another strange feeling. I used to fucking hate networking events. Today though, I don't think I mind too much. It used to be loud before Covid outside the room. The kind of hum that loads of people talking at the same time make. But the sound levels are down. HR used to organise training sessions on how to network at this kind of event. How to work a room, how to appear confident when you aren't, and how to get the most out of these events. All those kinds of soft skills. I remember one little pearl of advice from this training about how to introduce yourself to a small crowd of people when you don't know anyone. So, the advice in that situation (if I remember this correctly) is something along the lines of, 'in that instance, stride towards the group with one hand outstretched as if you have the intention of shaking hands with a member of the group, and introduce yourself'.

Never worked for me. Whenever I have to consciously think about doing something, there is a strong tendency for the rest of my bodily functions to suddenly stop working. So, in this instance, the brain would be telling the hand to stay outstretched, to go in for the hard handshake. But my power of speech would often disappear. You may have just delivered the most confident and firmest of handshakes known to man and gained a foothold into the group at the networking event, but you would then be talking like you have just had ten pints of Stella Artois.

The second problem with this approach is that people do not like being interrupted when they are mid-flow. They especially don't like to be introduced to someone they don't know when they are mid-flow. And finally, you will quickly and suddenly realise that with all the focus on the initial introduction, the breaking into the group, you will suddenly be in the middle of a group of strangers with not much to say.

No, my preferred method of 'pressing the flesh', in office worker parlance, at this kind of event is the classic 'smash and grab' technique. As far as I know, this isn't in any networking textbook. I may have made it up. The smash and grab technique involves targeting the sad loner on their own. Not the group. The individual. The billy-no-mates. One of the greatest miseries in life is being at a networking event, not knowing anyone, and standing in the middle of a room with only a coffee and vol-au-vent for company. You don't want to be that person. But someone has to be that person at every networking event. No matter how many people there are in the room, no matter how many little groups that room consists of, there is always someone, somewhere, who knows fewer people than you. It has many a time been me.

They are either standing next to the doors in case the billy-no-mates tag gets too much to bear and they need to leg it post-haste, or they hang around the buffet area for too long, acting like they are deciding whether to go for the pineapple and cheese sticks or the prawn sandwiches. They are using the finger buffet to kill time. Little sweat balls of stress drip down their faces into the complimentary prosecco as they pray for someone, anyone, to talk to them.

As I enter the room for today's networking session, there is an unusual feel. Less people. Less noise. A slightly nervy vibe. Some are masked up, some aren't. This is probably the new divide. There isn't much food though obviously. The finger buffet of the past would have been an incubator and spreader of office diseases. Just some sparkling water and some biscuits in packets.

I see a chap on his own in the corner. No mask on. That suits me. I had already got to the end of my tether with masks. I ran out ages ago. I had been spraying the same mask for the last few months with bleach spray.

He seems to be on his own. This is my way in. A quick, easy conversation. I reckon about ten minutes should do it. Management will hear about me making an effort. There is always some representative of Management at these events. You don't know who it is but the eyes and ears of Management are always hanging around. They won't have a clue who I am talking to. Could be a homeless man or Richard Branson's brother as far as they need to be concerned. As long as it isn't another employee of the company, that is all that is needed to gain a brownie point, to keep you ascending the greasy office pole, trampling on Felix while you are at it.

I bound over.

"Hello, how are you?" I ask without waiting for the reply. "What company are you from?" The second question follows in quick succession and really just to cement my arrival.

Strangely though, there is initial silence from this bloke. Just a fairly blank look. Indifference, bordering on hostility. There isn't the usual look of relief. There is no gratitude for being lifted out of loner status. This takes me slightly unawares.

"Dalton Rogers from the Dalton Brothers," he says quite clinically. There is no warmth at all in his reply.

Dalton Rogers from the the Dalton Brothers? *Really?*

"Ah so you are one of the owner of the business then?"

"How do you mean?"

Err. Not sure how to rephrase that one.

"So the name of your business. The Dalton Brothers. And your name being Dalton?"

"No nothing to do with me. I just work there."

Fuck me. Not only is his surname a first name, but his first name is the same name as the business that he doesn't have any stake in. I can see how this chap might be a bit pissed off.

"I am a stand-in though. Last-minute replacement. Not happy about it really. There's no benefit at all me being here. I am in the accounts department." Dalton carries on his moan.

Even worse. A member of the accounts department attending a networking event. What is the point in that?

More awkward silence. This is going badly. I take my phone out of my pocket, pretending to read an entirely fabricated text message.

"Oh, crikey, sorry about this. I have just had a customer text me with an urgent issue. Sorry, I will have to take my leave; duty calls, I am afraid. Nice to meet you anyway."

I am out of there.

62

Finger Buffet

The incident

We have been back in the office for a few weeks now. Hybrid working is in full flow. Some of the mask policies are a pain though. You don't need to wear masks at your desk, but you do need to wear them when on the move and in the office 'circulation areas'. Basically the circulation areas are the corridors. And there is never anyone in the corridors so I'm not quite sure of the logic behind that. However, I'm happy to do what is needed to keep Covid down.

The kitchen area is still out of bounds. The coffee machine was condemned a while ago. And there is definitely a bit more concern attending my usual sweaty, un-air-conditioned gym. Masks in there are frowned upon by most of the punters. I might bite the bullet and start going to the more health and safety conscious corporate gym.

I have been called into a HR meeting today. Not sure why. But it isn't Gertrude who has called it. Probably got something to do with that odd-looking chap who sat in with her at my last appraisal, before Covid, the one with the really limp-wristed handshake.

2.10pm

Sat in meeting room 7 waiting for HR. *Hurry up,* I think. *I haven't got all day.* They called the meeting for 2pm and I am still here waiting.

Suddenly the door opens and in comes a new person. Some bloke. Not seen him before.

"Hi Maxwell. Sorry to keep you," he says. "My name is Peter. How are you?"

"Yes, hello. Not too bad. Never thought I would say this, but actually quite glad to be back in the office," I say, all full of, actually not completely contrived enthusiasm.

"Can I introduce you to Karen, our new head of HR?"

A well-dressed lady emerges from behind this Peter character. Purple hair. Hold on *purple hair*? No fucking way. You are kidding me. It's only the well-dressed lady with the purple hair from the coffee house. The one Noah is obsessed with.

I can't quite believe it. She looks at me. I look at her. Her hand is outstretched. It suddenly occurs to me that she probably doesn't remember who I am. I mean, it was months ago that we met, and I was lying on the ground at the time. I have only really seen the bottom of her stilettos. I see if there is a flicker of acknowledgement. I hold her gaze slightly longer than usual as I shake her hand. No. Nothing going on there. If she does recognise me then she is doing a great job of covering it up.

"Hi Maxwell," she says. "Nice to meet you." Wait till I tell Noah.

"So Maxwell, this meeting is a follow-up to your previous appraisal," the purple-haired lady says, who I now know goes by the name of Karen. Wait til I tell Noah.

"I appreciate that that was in a different time, before lockdown and all that," she laughs.

Not sure that is the funniest joke I have heard today, but I chuckle along to not come across as impolite. Here we go again. The office game. The insincerity of it all. These are the bits I didn't miss during lockdown. But wait till I tell Noah about this. If she works here, then basically that means I know her e-mail. Before Noah will. Can't wait to gloat.

"So I think there was some reinforcement at that meeting that your performance indicators weren't quite where they should be."

"OK," I say.

"We have also had, as you probably would expect, a big drop in revenues as a result of the pandemic," the purple-haired lady says.

"Yes, I guess that would be right," I say.

"And the upshot of this is that as a company, we have had to consider all options to reduce the cost base."

Hang on. *Reduce the cost base*? That is fancy HR talk to mean people are either getting or about to be getting fired. And when I say people, given that these two are looking at me as they are saying it, that would be me in the firing line then. You have got to be kidding. These bastards are building up to sacking me. All dressed up in cost-cutting bullshit corporate speech.

How fucking dare they? I am going through the whole gamit of emotions. Fear, anger, upset, rage. All surging through me. And all the while I think the purple haired lady is still talking in the background. I have switched off. I don't need her to go further with this. I know where this is going. Is this finally the time to not be nice? Should I react here? The purple-haired lady is still talking in the background but I am not listening. The purple-haired lady from the coffee shop. She is now the controller of my destiny. How dare she go to my coffee shop? That's my fucking coffee house. Not hers. Heads of HR don't go there.

Is this a mistake? Has the purple-haired lady misunderstood why I was lying on the floor outside my coffee house that time? Did she really think I was some kind of pervert? Sacked because I had inadequate shoes on that day, or because Noah could never be arsed to grit his exit. Wait till I tell Noah all about all this.

It is about five minutes later. She is still talking. I am still not listening. After fifteen years of blood, sweat and tears given to this place. Always on time. Well, mostly. I've never ruffled anyone's feathers that didn't need ruffling. And what do I get for all that? The bottom of the purple-haired lady's stilettos. Again.

Go on, say it. Go on, I dare you. Tell me I am sacked. They are still going round the houses. It would be much easier for everyone if they just get to the point.

"So it's with a heavy heart that we are going to have to let you go."

Oh, there you go. Finally.

"We really appreciate your commitment and dedication to the company over the years, and we will make sure you are well compensated for a period of time."

I have two options. Either get down on my knees and plead, or launch myself at them across the desk.

In the end I don't take either option. I just get up, quite calmly and in a measured manner. For some reason I bring my hand up to my head, saluting them. There is a slight look of bewilderment on their faces. I am not sure if I see the man's hand under the table. What is his name – Peter, Paul? Can't quite remember. Who gives a toss though? Whatever his name is, he looks like he is about to press the red panic button. I then click my heels, turn around and take my leave. I deliberately leave the door open.

63

Hair of the Dog?

Wednesday, 11am Locked-down again

Today is the day after being sacked. Sacked from the company I have devoted most of my office working life to. Not even given any kind of severance pay. Just some statutory pay bullshit. Covid apparently. Fucking Covid.

So all that means, understandably I think, that I have just woken up with the mother of all hangovers. It is a return to lockdown for me then. Back to the office didn't last very long. I am now on permanent lockdown. Permanent lockdown due to my non-consensual exclusion from the company for, well, the rest of my life.

I check around for my mobile. Where is it? Where the fuck is it? Did I find Management's number, or Peter's, or the purple-haired lady's, and send some inappropriate stuff through? Some stuff that, sacking or no sacking, I will be regretting for the foreseeable?

There it is. My phone. Under a half-eaten cheese and beetroot sandwich. I check the sent items. Looks OK. No violence threatened on anyone.

There is a message though. 6.30am. From Wendy. It just says: *When you get over your hangover call me xx*

I take some paracetamol and go back to sleep. It isn't as if I have anywhere to go.

64

The Notebook

Part II

3pm

I got up at 2.30 today. No shame in that. It's still not like I have anywhere to be, except probably the dole office shortly.

I am sat again at my throne of contemplation. The chair in the kitchen. I think I will phone Wendy a bit later. I haven't even spoken to her about her dad properly yet. I could do with Wendy right about now. My angst is still being channelled at the HR pallbearers who broke the news to me. How are they sleeping at night? And the purple-haired lady from the coffee house. Noah would be fuming. Sticking up for his mate. Taking my side. Or maybe he would still be salivating over the purple-haired lady, in the same way as when he didn't notice that I had gone arse over tit when she was last present.

I still can't believe I am now sat again in my kitchen. First lockdown, and then the chop.

This morning, just a few short hours earlier, I had dug out my notebook. The one I started after Lennox told me to write shit down. My thoughts, ideas, positive words, recriminations – anything really. The only rule of the notebook is that it has to mean something. Good or bad, it has to mean something. It is in front of me on the coffee table. There is nothing else on the table. Just this notepad and my cup of tea.

There is lot in this notepad that I probably don't want to read now. Stuff to be avoided in my current emotional state. But there is other stuff too. Maybe I can find inspiration in this. I open it up and start reading.

There must be something here. I need something.

Don't be the man too stupid to not take advice from those more experienced than you.

Doesn't really help in my current situation.

There is always someone richer than you.

That's currently rubbing salt in the wounds.

No one can carry the weight of the world on their shoulders. Just carry what you need to.

Not sure where that one came from. Was that me? Was it Noah? Was it from a teacher from school? I don't even remember that. Getting closer maybe.

If you can face triumph and disaster and treat those two imposters just the same.

I pause for a second. That's one that Noah has ripped right off of Rudyard Kipling.

It wasn't the best of times, it wasn't the worst of times. Another Noah rip off. And not just a rip off, but a misquoted rip off. I must be reading from the section in my notepad headed 'Misquoted rip-off thoughts of the day from Noah'. I move on.

When frying mushrooms, don't move them for the first five minutes.

Eh? That isn't a thought for the day. That is a note from a cooking recipe. That is in the wrong section.

Despots think that putting a tie on gives them respectability, legitimacy, even though most despots are generally under five feet tall and therefore have little man syndrome.

Again, I must be in the wrong section. That will be another one for *The Alien Jury*.

This might not quite be working. This might not be the time for this kind of self-reflection. Everything is still a bit too raw. This might be an exercise for another day. I chuck the notepad off the table. It sticks to the bottom of the wall.

65

Sometimes You Can't Make it on Your Own

7pm (the same day)
Wendy

My mobile is ringing. I have fallen asleep at my kitchen table, face full into a bowl of All Bran.

"Hello." I answer it without even checking who it is. I am half asleep still.

"Jesus, Max, are you only just waking up?" comes a familiar, calm, reassuring voice. It is Wendy.

"Eh up, you," I say, just about coming round. "Sobered up yet then, Max? Or are you still in the throwing up stage?"

"Eh? Don't know what you mean. I was sober as anything last night."

"Oh OK, I believe you."

"Anyway, Wendy, I have some stuff to tell you. But before I do, how are you doing? Can't believe about your dad. Are you doing OK?"

"Yeah I am OK, Max. It was a shock, but the family are rallying around."

"I really liked your dad."

"He wasn't in much pain, so that helps." "Anything I can do, obviously, Wendy."

"I know, Max. You told me all this last night."

"Eh?"

"Not drunk? My arse you weren't. And listen, to avoid you having to go through the pain of telling me you have got the sack from work again you needn't bother, as you went through all that last night also."

"I did? Jesus, I must have had more than I thought." I sigh. "So I'm a bit at sea with it all, Wendy, to be honest. Just can't believe they are treating me like that. They are just using this pandemic as a smokescreen. Time to get rid of some dead wood. Me being the dead wood."

"Listen Max, I know this is tough at the moment. I really do. And I am not saying this isn't a problem. You know, this redundancy. But I need to tell you something that might be a little hard to hear. Some home truths."

"OK," I say.

"So, Max, the thing is, and there is no easy way of saying this, but you haven't been committed to that job for a long time. For a really long time."

"OK," I say, slightly confused. "But I have only ever worked there, Wendy."

"Yeah, you have always physically worked there. But in the last few years you have been... how can I put this, Max? On a bit of a mental walkabout."

"It hasn't been easy you know, Wendy. Going through all that shit with Mandy, and with Evie also. Jesus Christ, Wendy, with Evie as well," I say, my voice cracking slightly.

"I know Max. I know. You know I know. If anyone does it is me. But it isn't just all that stuff, Max. Its been going on longer than that. It goes deeper than that." Wendy pauses. "So on your job, Max. Maybe this is a positive for you."

"Wendy, we are in a pandemic still. I am not a millionaire, you know. I still have bills to pay like anyone else."

"I understand that. But you have to take something from this. I just think you haven't been committed to that job from the first day you set foot in the building. In fact, you haven't been committed to office work since the first time I saw you completely unable to tie your work tie. You still can't. And you know why you can't tie your tie?"

"'Cos it is quite a technical piece of clothing."

"No Maxwell. It's because you don't want to learn how to tie it. And you know why you don't want to learn how to tie the tie? Because you don't like what it represents. Desks, offices, being told what to do. You are more of a nomad than that."

"Nomad?"

"Yes, a nomad. A nomad. Restless. Generally nomads don't work in offices. Maybe this sacking is a good thing. Maybe this is life's way of giving you a good old boot up the jacksey."

"Err, not quite sure what a nomad is, Wendy. Is that like being in the French Foreign Legion?"

"You know what my dad said when he was on his way out, Maxwell? He said 'You only appreciate living when you can start to see the end" – You need to get out there Max. Maybe I do to…"

Wendy's voice is cracking slightly now. She is struggling. I am not used to hearing Wendy struggling. There isn't much I can say to that. I pause for a bit. So does she. Not an uncomfortable pause. A pause between two mates who have known each other forever.

"Yeah, he is right, Wendy. Course he is. Your dad, I mean. God bless him. But I am trying, you know."

"I know you are, Max," she says calmly. "So am I."

And just one more thing, Max.

"Please stop now, Wendy. Not sure how much more of this I can take."

Wendy laughs.

"Make sure you have bought some more hedge cutters for when I am back."

And with that she hangs up.

I stare ahead for a minute, and then suddenly start crying. I don't usually cry. But I can't quite control it. It comes out of nowhere.

I'm still crying about five minutes later. I am a wreck.

Last Chapter

A Few Days Later

The Screwtape letters

Two days after the call from Wendy, I'm sat at my table again. I have been to bed in the meantime though.

I have been thinking about what Wendy was saying. And then thought about it some more. And I've been thinking about nothing else really for the past two days. 'Stop living in your head.' I think that is what Wendy was saying to me. Have I been doing that? Obsessing, over-analysing, self-recriminating, self-indulging, wallowing?

The notebook is back on the middle of the table. It took a little while to prise it from the wall after I lobbed it the other day.

The notebook is open. I have my old fountain pen from school. The one with the broken nib. I have spent some time trying to fix it. I need it fixed. I want a pen with some history behind it. A pen that has some meaning behind it. Some resonance. Because there will never, ever be anything more important for me to write than what I am about to write now.

Letters. That's what I am about to write. Letters. Letters that mean something to me. Hopefully they might mean something to anyone that might read them in future. As long as this notepad survives, then so will my letters. And so far, for all my tantrums, this notepad has just about stayed in one piece.

These will be my screwtape letters. Or maybe the office equivalent. The Sellotape letters.

I start writing…

Letter number 1

Dear Noah,

My friend, I would like to start this letter on a sour note. I still haven't forgiven you for humiliating me on that dating website. Forgiveness takes time, and even if I do manage to get to forgiveness island, your actions won't ever be forgotten. They are indelibly and forever etched on my brain, and that poor girl Samantha's, who was subjected to such barbarism. No-one wants to see me wearing shorts and a shirt over the internet. How dare you force that on someone.

Having got that off my chest, if you are reading this then you need to know I am not currently in the coffee house. I am taking a break from the coffee and banter for a while. Just off to, well, dream it all up again. No shame in that. And no shame in admitting I was wrong. I can't always be right. You my friend, were right. I did need a break. Not in Magaluf though you tosser. I need a slightly more cultural break than that, I feel. Our lads' week will have to be put on hold just for a bit. But when I have had my wander, I promise we will one day be side by side on a big inflatable somewhere hot, sipping piña coladas with those little umbrellas in them. You won't be serving me any drinks. I will be getting my own. And I promise you my shadow will be firmly where it should be, following me around for the ride.

What you might not know though, Noah my friend, is that in some of my slightly bleaker moments, your banter and your thoughts for the day really did keep me going. Thank you for that.

Yours Maxwell

P.S. Touch my arse again and I am going to the police.

Letter number 2

Dear Lennox,

I trust this letter find you well. Hopefully you are proud of me as it was you who told me to 'write shit down' a while back. You were right. Writing stuff down is cathartic. Therapeutic. It is a way to organise your thoughts. For all the great advice you gave me, I would have paid the money just for that piece of advice alone.

I hope business is going well, if you are even still in the therapy game. If not I hope you find your niche, but there are not many people in this world who master the skill of listening, really listening, instead of just talking.

I have been thinking long and hard about it and I think I might have finally realised why I can

never get to sheep number sixteen. But I will tell
you the answer when I see you.
Probably your worst patient ever, Maxwell

Letter number 3

Dear Jim from Accounts
I have come to realise that it is entirely not your
fault that I was really bad at my times tables at
school, and that as such I have developed a chronic
and deep-seated fear of figures and numbers.
All my fault. Catch you again some day on the
8.08 train.
Maxwell Orwellian

Letter number 4

Dear Covid 19,
Fuck you.
Maxwell Orwellian

Letter number 5

Dear Wendy,
I really don't know where to start, Wendy. So I am
going to start at the beginning. Because that's where
you came in. At the start. You were always there. You
have always been there. I had no right to any of that. I
should have been more there for you. Our relationship
is like some kind of uneven see-saw. I am the fat chap
on one side, letting you take all my weight.

But I need to continue to be a bit selfish. Just for the time being. You pushed me in this direction and you were right. I need to find a bit of a different path for the moment. Not quite sure what it is. But I know what it isn't. Not the office. Not for the foreseeable anyway. I will let you know where I am just as soon as I get there.

Love Max Xx

P.S. I will sort out some new hedge cutters soon.

Letter number 6

Dear Maxwell,

A few weeks ago, if I was going to write a letter to you, there would have been a lot of swearing in it. A lot of stuff like, 'get a grip you useless bastard', or 'sort your beard out', or 'stop letting Wendy's garden get so overgrown'. Not that that is all suddenly wrong. That would just be the tip of the iceberg. But I have realised something. Just very recently actually. With Wendy's help. I may actually need to consider being a little kinder to you myself. Look at some positives. Some stuff that I have done that I would be, I don't know… well, a bit proud of. The little things. Helping that new starter when she was floundering around not being able to operate the photocopier. Not much in itself. But it is the little things.

So you got upset about being sacked. Put it into perspective, Maxwell you big bastard. Get some perspective and grow bigger balls whilst you are at it. So I am trying to tell you Maxwell, my future self, to take a break. Travel the world. Drink some unusual beer in some far off part of the world. You are still just about young enough to do it. In addition you need to work on doing the following things for the rest of your life.

1. *Stop letting other people's bodily functions bother you.*
2. *Find Lennox.*
3. *Actually fly in person and for real to Australia and not on a computer flight simulator at home whilst wearing a pilots uniform bought off Amazon.*
4. *Travel a bit. Surprise Evie in the south of France.*
5. *Embrace who you are and become a digital nomad.*
6. *Do more charity work.*
7. *Maybe try different careers. Pottery maker, labourer, window cleaner, wrestler, French Foreign Legion. As long as it doesn't involve sitting in an office, or wearing a tie.*
8. *Possibly, and provided insurance is relatively affordable, get a dog.*
9. *Finally discover the truth about helium balloons.*

Find stuff you like about yourself. If you can't find anything to like then sure as shit no one else will. And despite yourself, no man is an island. I realised that and more during a pandemic-induced lockdown. The world might be going mad, but as long as there enough good people, as long as the good people outweigh the bad, then we will all be in Bob Marley land, and that my friend, is not a bad place to be.

Yours in complete sincerity for once, Maxwell

Final letter

Dear Evie,

I hope you are having the best time darling. That's what you should be doing. Having the best time. Wherever you are reading this.

I am not actually sure if you will ever read this letter. I am not sure if I want you to read it. Maybe this letter is as much for me as it is for you. You are a free spirit. You always were. I knew that from the day I held you in my arms when you came into this world. You weren't even really crying if I remember. Most babies do, I think. But you didn't really. You already had a calmness that I have never had. That's the place I am trying to get to. Calmness Town.

You don't need any advice from me, so I will keep this letter short. All I would ever say is this. If I have learnt anything over forty-two years or so of being in this world it is probably this: always follow your own path. Not a path that someone

else has laid for you. You know the route you are
on better than anyone else.
You were always the best thing about me.
Always will be.
Love always, Yer Dad

So maybe the journey for me doesn't end here. Maybe it starts here. Fuck the past, kiss the future. Experience is overrated. It is time to get back to innocence. Close the gap. Make Ivan The Pisshead proud.

Funny how life can pan out. It has taken a worldwide pandemic, being sacked from work by the purple haired lady who had been flirting with my mate for a while, a boot up the arse from Wendy, and an insight from a homeless man for me to wake up and smell the tulips. Grab this one in a billion chance called your life and do what you should with it.

Jettison the excess baggage. A bit like exceeding your baggage allowance on your flight to Magaluf. Lob the vodka, condoms and spare pairs of boxers. The unnecessaries. Keep the essentials. Not many of them are physical things as it turns out. God only knows where it is going to take me, and I don't know whether it will one way or a return. But I am on board. And that, in the end, is really all that matters.

(As long as Jim from accounts isn't sat next to me…)

Epilogue

The Ballad of
the Office Worker

In the end I wasn't one of them. An office worker, that is. I found another way. I wasn't really an office worker at any point. Not that I regret it all. The rich tapestry of life. And the HR assassins that ended it all probably knew that too. I have long made peace with them. I hope Noah and the purple-haired lady have a beautiful future together.

I am not sure I would have chosen to be an office worker from birth. You know when your parents first sit you down at about eight and ask you what you want to do with the rest of your life? I am not so sure that at that point I would have said, 'Daddy I want to be sat at a desk in front of a computer all my life and be an office worker'.

But I want to end this by penning a final ode to office workers. Not with my fountain pen. In print. In modern, contemporary font. The way office workers in the future would want it. So this is a 'cheers' to the office worker. Wherever they are. Maybe not considered keyworkers in the heat of a pandemic, but a vital part of society.

Two years spent ironing shirts. Three years trying to figure out how to put a tie on. One and a half years with your head buried in the stationery cupboard. Three years sat in meetings. One month sat in productive meetings. One year worrying about the threat of redundancy. Five minutes actually being made redundant. Eight months spent on the photocopier (with another three months in the queue for the photocopier). Six months in appraisal meetings. Three months in the office lift. One week stuck in office lifts that have broken down. One year flirting with the opposite sex. One year getting rejected by the opposite sex.

Office workers may well be at a much greater risk than the majority of the population for diseases brought about by being sedentary for most of the day. Office workers may be stooping by the time they are in their early to mid-forties. It is possible that given the lifestyle issues that the office throws up, office working may well in the future be listed amongst the top five most dangerous professions in the world.

So what truly lies in the future of the office worker? Supermarkets might be replacing till workers with self-scanners. Robots might be starting to take over building buildings. But I haven't yet seen a robot in a suit making his way to the office. Not quite yet, anyway.

Modern day gladiators keeping the wheels of commerce turning. There may not be many gravestones that have an epitaph to their life as office workers carved into the headstones. But if you are yourself an office worker then you should be proud to revel in your status. Stand tall. Know that you, yes you, are a fundamental cog in the commercial world.

They say the only thing you can see from space is the Chinese Wall. That may be. But at just about 8.50 in the morning, if ET had his binoculars out, he would see wave upon wave of office workers making their honest way to work, like a swarm of ants. Each one telling their own unique story, their perspective on the office.

When it is 16 January and it is pissing it down outside, your computer keeps crashing and that office bonus is as far away as the moon, when you are at your most irritated, or most bored, or most angry, then take heart in this thought: after another twenty years, you will be eligible to cash in your final salary pension.

But when the alien invasion comes and the leaders of the free world look to mobilise the largest collective class of human beings on the planet, all they need to do is to call on the office workers of the world to unite. Those aliens would be sent packing. The human network. The most powerful of things.

Now where did I put my tie?

Author biography

As a lawyer Kieron Crowther has been soliciting his whole working life, apart from a stint working as a labourer for his father in law, which didn't really work out.

He lives with his beautiful family, one cat and kitten that don't really get on, and a few garden fish (Although he hasn't seen his fish in a while).

He has a keen interest in politics, and is looking at a possible new career as leader of the Bullshit Party.

He does, however, remain an office worker to this day.

 Matador

For exclusive discounts on Matador titles,
sign up to our occasional newsletter at
troubador.co.uk/bookshop